DRAGON FORCE

INFINITY'S SECRET

Also by
KATIE & KEVIN TSANG

DRAGON REALM series

DRAGON MOUNTAIN

DRAGON LEGEND

DRAGON CITY

DRAGON RISING

DRAGON DESTINY

DRAGON FORCE series

INFINITY'S SECRET

DRAGON FORCE

INFINITY'S SECRET

KATIE & KEVIN TSANG

SIMON & SCHUSTER

First published in Great Britain in 2023 by Simon & Schuster UK Ltd

1 3 5 7 9 10 8 6 4 2

Simon & Schuster UK Ltd
1st Floor, 222 Gray's Inn Road
London
WC1X 8HB

www.simonandschuster.co.uk
www.simonandschuster.com.au
www.simonandschuster.co.in

Simon & Schuster Australia, Sydney
Simon & Schuster India, New Delhi

A CIP catalogue record for this book is available from the British Library.

PB ISBN 978-1-3985-2012-7
eBook ISBN 978-1-3985-2014-1
eAudio ISBN 978-1-3985-2013-4

Typeset in the UK by M Rules

Printed and bound in the UK using 100% Renewable
Electricity at CPI Group (UK) Ltd

For our daughters,
Evie and Mira

DRAGON'S CLAW

THE LABS

UNDERWATER JUNGLE

VOLCANO

CLAW BEACH

DRACORDIA

A Song of Warning

Beyond the stars, a creature is stirring.

It can smell something that it wants. Something far away but delicious. It can almost taste the magic in the air. And it is hungry. So very, very hungry.

But what it wants is a long distance away. It will be a long journey. Yet the creature knows the trip will be worth it. It will follow the scent until it gets what it wants.

This creature is always ravenous. No matter how much it devours, it is never satisfied. It could swallow everything in its path and still want more. And it will not stop.

The creature stretches and snarls, and as it does,

the stars in the sky shake, frightened of what is coming, scared of what they cannot stop. And so they begin to sing a song of warning, a song that only few can hear.

In a world changed for ever by the arrival of magic and dragons, there is music in the air; a quiet humming that only few can hear.

A young dragon hears it, and recognizes the alarm. She tilts her head and listens, and hopes that the one she is seeking can hear it too.

Dragons in the Woods

Lance Lo was used to seeing dragons.

He usually spotted them with his younger sister, Zoe, when they walked home from school through the woods. They lived with their parents in a small red house on a busy street, in an even busier city, but behind their house were the woods. Woods where they played, but also where dragons had chosen to make their home.

Lance and Zoe knew, as all children did, to be respectful towards the dragons and to let them approach you first. Most dragons that lived in human-populated areas were friendly after all. But on the off-chance that a dragon became aggressive, which was unlikely but had happened, they knew they could blow their emergency whistle to call the Dragon Force for help.

Lance had only needed to use his emergency whistle once before – two years ago when he and Zoe had accidentally woken up a sleeping rock dragon. The rock dragon had not been pleased, and when it'd roared its displeasure, snapping its giant jaws at Lance, he'd been frozen with fear for a moment, before remembering that this was the very reason he wore the whistle everywhere he went.

Moments later, a beautiful blue and green dragon with giant yellow wings had appeared from a portal and swiftly subdued the rock dragon. Lance tried to thank the rescuing dragon, but it flew off before he could say anything. As it did, Lance noticed that it wore a Dragon Force pendant around its neck.

The Dragon Force was the global protection unit, created five years ago when dragons and humans had first been forced to live together in what was now known as the New World. Led by Billy Chan, who was only seventeen years old, and his dragon, Spark, the Dragon Force consisted of a small group of human heroes and their dragon counterparts who had saved the world when the hidden Dragon Realm had crashed into the Human Realm. They protected humans from dangerous dragons, dragons from dangerous humans, and, most of all, humans and dragons from their shared enemies, of which there were more every day.

Because dragons weren't the only creatures to enter the Human Realm; dangerous beasts had found their way in too. Lance had seen reports of huge two-headed scorpions, giant grasshoppers with metal pincers and razor-sharp wings, flying fish that could swallow aeroplanes, and even a rampaging squid the size of a town. And these new creatures had no interest in building relationships with humans *nor* dragons. That's where the Dragon Force came in.

Lance had never forgotten the dragon that saved him and his sister from the grumpy rock dragon. It was like meeting a real-life superhero. And from that moment, it became his mission to one day join the Dragon Force and protect those who needed it most.

But after that day, to his secret disappointment, he hadn't needed to call upon the Dragon Force again.

Most of the dragons he and Zoe saw in the woods ignored them. The speckled dragon spent most of its time curled up in the top branches of trees, peering down at people passing by. Dragons also settled all over the neighbourhood. The maroon dragon who lived outside the woods above the cheese shop was friendly, and if you brought it sweets, it would sometimes tell you a story. There was even a tiny pink dragon who loved cars, and when someone had car trouble, it was usually because the pink dragon was sleeping under the bonnet.

Lance and Zoe lived in London, or at least where London used to be, as the world they once knew no longer existed. When the Dragon Realm fell into the Human Realm, the two realms became one, for ever altering the landscape. Humans and dragons referred to it as the Great Collapse, and for the first year, the maps changed almost daily. New rivers, mountain ranges and even entire continents appeared out of nowhere, and the world itself grew, making room for new lands. Physicists and geologists were baffled – the rules that humans had lived by for so long were no more.

On top of that, dragons brought dragon magic, and that meant nothing was ever quite as it seemed. Sometimes Lance couldn't believe he had to go to school and learn things like grammar and chemistry when there were real dragons with superpowers flying around.

So it wasn't out of the ordinary for them to see the shadow of a dragon overhead on their walk home on the last day of school before the summer holidays.

At twelve, Lance was two years older than his sister Zoe, and he told all his friends that the reason they walked home together was so he could look after her, but the truth was it was also because he felt safer with her by his side. As they walked, he noted the dragon overhead – its long shadow and the whoosh of air that signalled it was flying low. But it had flown by too fast for Lance to make out any other details, which was a shame because he liked to record every new dragon in his dragon notebook. This one probably wasn't even new, he told himself. It was most likely the speckled one out for an afternoon flight. But then the dragon turned around and flew closer and lower, and Lance saw that it was indeed a new dragon.

It was lavender-coloured, with a long and slender snake-like body. It had dozens of gossamer wings, all different sizes and shapes, and, interestingly, asymmetrical, in a way that Lance had never seen before. It looked a little like a wildflower that had taken flight, and there was a sweet scent in the air, like the smell of roses. Lance swayed on his feet and found he couldn't quite look away, almost as if he had been hypnotized.

And then the dragon swooped right towards them, and Lance broke out of the trance.

'Zoe! Get back!' cried Lance, leaping in front of his sister. He fumbled for his whistle, but it wasn't round his neck. Where was it? Was it in his backpack? His pocket?

The dragon was almost upon them, so close now that he could see its bright purple eyes above a long snout sprouting with whiskers. Lilac-coloured smoke curled out of its nostrils.

Why couldn't he find his whistle? 'Zoe! Do you have your whistle? Quick!'

But Zoe didn't move, staring at the approaching lavender dragon with an expression of awe. The dragon swooped around Lance and flew near to Zoe, so close it appeared to be smelling her hair. Its eyes began to glow.

'Stay away from her!' said Lance, whacking the dragon with his backpack.

The dragon didn't seem to notice. There was a rush of wind, and before Lance realized what was happening, Zoe was propelled up into the air, and landed on the dragon's back.

Lance leaped up, trying to grab the dragon's tail to clamber up after her. 'Don't take my sister!' he cried. 'Zoe, don't worry!'

But Zoe wasn't afraid. She was beaming. 'Lance! I think . . . I think this is my dragon! I can feel it!'

Lance was so startled that he stumbled backwards and fell, hard, on his backside. As he stared up at his sister, and the dragon she was riding, he saw the telltale gold charge running from Zoe's heart to the dragon's heart. Lance gasped. He had heard about this, about what happened when a dragon and a human found that their hearts matched, but he had never seen a heart bond form before. The heart bond linked the dragon and human for ever, granting them both power. And it was the thing Lance wanted more than anything – a heart-bonded dragon of his own.

Here, right in the woods by their house, was a dragon who had sought out Zoe and awoken the heart bond between them. Zoe closed her eyes, her expression one of utter bliss, and a moment later the dragon gently landed next to Lance, who was still staring, gobsmacked. Zoe slid off the dragon's back, as if she'd done it hundreds of times before.

'I will see you at Camp Claw,' said the dragon. And then, with a burst of speed, it disappeared into the sky, leaving only the lingering scent of flowers behind.

Resilient Creatures

Zoe's dark eyes shone with joy as she bounced up and down, almost bursting with excitement.

'Can you believe it, Lance? My dragon found me! I wonder how it tracked me down. Oh, isn't it the most beautiful dragon you've ever seen? And it said it would see me at Camp Claw! I didn't even know you could go to Camp Claw before you were twelve – did you? Have you heard of anyone younger going? Do you think I might be the youngest human ever to go?'

The aptly named camp was located in the most magical and mythical place in the New World – Dragon's Claw, a peninsula off Dracordia, a brand-new continent that had emerged in the Pacific Ocean during the Great Collapse. This was also where the Dragon Force was based. Camp Claw was where children identified as having the potential to form exceptionally strong heart bonds were invited to learn more about dragons. Some who were invited were already heart-bonded, but most came without one. The camp tried to find bonds for those who didn't have them. And for those who did, they trained with their dragons and developed their newfound powers. Ultimately, those who proved themselves worthy were invited to join the elite Dragon Force.

Heart bonds weren't that common in the New World, even though humans and dragons had been living together in the same realm for five years. This didn't surprise Lance particularly. After all, to form a heart bond, you needed to find a dragon whose heart matched your own exactly. Sometimes a dragon would get a *feeling* that would lead it to its human. Other times, it was the human who sought out the dragon. And, of course, often it was luck, where the two matching hearts were in the same place at the same time, awakening the bond.

But hearts were as mysterious as they were astonishing. Feeling the beat of his own heart in his chest, Lance just hoped that somewhere there was a dragon who had a heart that matched his own. As Zoe now did.

He grinned at his sister and ruffled her hair. 'Let's get home,' he said. 'I can't wait for you to tell Mum and Dad!'

'I'm sure you'll find a heart bond too,' Zoe said.

Lance's smile faltered. 'Maybe.'

He was proud of his sister, he really was, but suddenly he was worried that maybe he wouldn't be as lucky as her.

What if he never found his dragon?

What if he didn't *have* a dragon?

He tried to put the thoughts out of his head as he hurried Zoe along the path through the woods back to their house.

Later that night, after Zoe had breathlessly told their incredulous parents what had happened, the whole family had celebrated with Zoe's favourite meal: wok-fried noodles with spicy shrimp. Lance had kept a smile on his face throughout the story, even when his mum had pointedly asked if a dragon had found him too.

'Not today!' he'd said cheerfully. 'But what are the chances of two dragons showing up on the same day?'

His dad, however, was worried about what the dragon had said about Camp Claw. He kept scratching his head and muttering about how Zoe was too young to go off on her own to a camp run by dragons. 'She's only ten, for goodness' sake. Dragon or no dragon, I'm not sending my daughter to a camp on the other side of the globe!'

But they all knew, of course, that Zoe would be going to Camp Claw when the time came. Nobody said no to a dragon. And on top of that, their dad never said no to Zoe.

The big question was, when would she be going? Camp Claw always took place over the summer, Lance knew that much, but he wasn't sure exactly when. And there was the even bigger question of how she would get to Camp Claw. Supposedly campers went by portal, but that only added to the uncertainty.

Lance had never been in a portal, and they made

him nervous. As far as he understood it, only a few dragons had the ability to create portals. Humans hadn't yet worked out how to produce them on their own. But how did you know the portal would take you to the location you were expecting? And, more importantly, how did you know it was a safe portal to take? What if you got stuck, or only half of you made it through? Or what if it wasn't a portal at all but a sneaky trap? It wasn't as if there was a well-known portal system that everyone used and trusted like they did aeroplanes, at least not yet. To Lance, stepping into a portal was like a high-stakes trust fall exercise. Except, instead of falling into someone's arms, you were falling into a potentially endless pit. The rational part of Lance's brain told him that Zoe was going to be fine, but he couldn't help but worry about his sister. Portals were still relatively new to humans after all.

'Why does the whole thing need to be shrouded in secrecy anyway?' their dad went on. 'It isn't as if we don't know about the existence of dragons! Why can't I drop off my daughter at dragon camp, like . . . I don't know . . . swim camp?'

'Dad!' Zoe exclaimed. 'Of course you can't drop me off. That would be so embarrassing! It's *Camp Claw*, the most amazing camp in the *entire world* that *everyone* wants to go to! Anyone can go to swim camp. Only the most special humans are invited to Camp Claw!'

Lance winced and stared down at his noodles. It was true, in a way. He had heard that the leader of Camp Claw and her dragon were able to sense new heart bonds around the world and could tell which humans had the most potential to develop exceptionally strong powers.

Zoe slurped up more of her noodles and kept talking. 'Aren't you proud of me?'

'Of course we're proud,' their dad quickly said. 'I know how much you love dragons.' He glanced at Lance, who was pushing his food around his bowl, his appetite suddenly gone. 'Both of you.'

Lance's mum patted his hand. 'I'm sure your dragon will come soon, sweetie.'

Lance forced a smile. He knew his parents were trying to help. 'Don't worry about me! It's Zoe's night!'

But part of him agreed with his dad. Surely Zoe

was too young to go to Camp Claw? He always looked out for his little sister. How was he going to do that if they were apart? It wasn't just that he felt a little jealous – he was worried about her too.

Ever since Zoe was born, Lance had taken his role as big brother very seriously. His earliest memories were of her – a tiny Zoe toddling around after him wherever he went. And as they grew older, they stayed close. Zoe always wanted to join in when he played football with his friends, and she was his biggest supporter when it came to his musical performances. Lance had friends who complained about their younger siblings, but he genuinely liked hanging out with his sister. She made everyone laugh, and she was constantly excited and full of energy. And she was fearless in a way that he truly admired. Plus, it was nice to have someone he knew would always be on his side. Sure, they bickered over silly things, but he could count on Zoe more than anyone.

The two of them even looked similar. They both had dark brown hair with just a little bit of a wave in it, and wide dark eyes that crinkled in the corners when they smiled. They were a combination of their dad, who was Chinese and had straight black hair, and their mum, who was English and had fair skin, light-brown curly hair and freckles. If Zoe had been slightly taller, they could have been mistaken for twins.

But now Zoe had a heart bond, it felt as if *she* was the older sibling who would be looking after Lance. He wasn't sure how he felt about that. He knew he was happy for his sister, as the only person who loved dragons more than he did, but the situation made him anxious.

'Lance is right – this is my night! It's like all my birthdays rolled into one,' Zoe said, tucking her dark hair behind her ears. 'Oooh, can we have cake? After all, this is *way* more special than a birthday! A birthday happens every year, but you only get the call up to go to Camp Claw once in a lifetime!'

Their mum smiled. 'I don't know about cake, but let me see if we have any ice cream. You're right – this is a very special occasion.'

Not every family was overjoyed if their child received an invitation for Camp Claw. Five years ago, most of the population hadn't even believed in dragons. There had always been some humans who'd known about the existence of dragons though. That was where the stories had first come from. But reading about dragons in a book and seeing one on your doorstep were very different things.

The first year after the dragons arrived had been the hardest. Lance still remembered how afraid everyone had been. Every day had uncovered a new terrifying discovery and the political debate about whether dragons were friend or foe had been endless.

And throughout it all, six human children, who now led the Dragon Force, had stood strong alongside dragons, despite being the same age that Lance was now. They'd fought to prove that the world was better off with these creatures in it. And more than that, that humanity needed dragons to survive as a species.

However, not every dragon was friendly towards humans, and the world quickly found places for those dragons who wanted to live out their days without encountering humankind. Remote jungles, icy mountains and deep ocean trenches were where most of these dragons went.

But when Dracordia was discovered, it became the go-to place for dragons who wanted to roam in peace. They were followed by brave humans who were drawn to dragons, even the more aggressive ones, setting up a few small settlements on the new continent.

Some humans in Dracordia and the wider world became dragon-obsessed. They worshipped them, built temples in their honour and fell to their knees every time a dragon flew overhead. The dragons seemed amused by this, and some took great delight in flying over the temples and showing off their powers.

The New World certainly brought about some positive changes. Dragons were more advanced in almost every way, and the ones who liked humans shared their knowledge and their magic, allowing huge gains to be made in medicine and technology.

But other humans grew to fear dragons. They set up human-only enclaves where no talk of the creatures was allowed, erected giant steel domes so they'd never accidentally see a dragon in flight and taught their children to hate dragonkind.

For a time, there had even been groups who had believed they could hunt dragons and use their body parts to create their own magic. But when a dragon died, its magic died with it. The global dragon delegation had soon issued warnings that dragon poaching would lead to retaliation. The message had been loud and clear: if humanity wanted to survive in the New World, they needed to learn to live alongside dragons in peace, or as close to peace as possible.

It was an uneasy treaty, but what did come out of it was that almost all human countries had ceased war against each other because they now had bigger issues to deal with. Humanity had bonded in a way never before seen in history, and they had dragons to thank for it. Dragons didn't side with any one country, or respect arbitrary boundary lines; they had their own strange moral compass that was hard to understand, but they tended to trust children more than adults.

A year after the Great Collapse, a new kind of

normal emerged. Most humans tried to carry on life as they'd known it, just with the addition of dragons. Lance's parents had done that. They'd stayed living in London, even as London changed. His mum still worked as a music teacher, his dad was still a food scientist but with the occasional dragon colleague. Dragons were very good at science on the whole, and *very* interested in food.

Lance felt like his three great passions in life were music, food and dragons. He had his parents to thank for the first two, but his dragon obsession had been fully organic. Not that he was alone in that feeling. Almost everyone he knew yearned for a heart bond.

After Zoe's celebration dinner, Lance headed upstairs to his room. He still couldn't quite believe his sister had a heart bond. He'd always imagined them both having one, and he'd get his first as the eldest. When it came to Lance and Zoe, he'd always gone first.

Until now.

He was proud of her, he really was, but it was a lot to process. So he did what he always found himself doing when he needed to think things through – he took out his violin.

Lance also played the piano and guitar, but the violin was his favourite. His mum had made sure he knew how to play an instrument from an early age, and he'd taken to it right away. He didn't even mind the hours of practice. He found it soothing, and it was rewarding seeing his slow but steady improvement.

It was late, so Lance was careful to play quietly, but he still let himself get lost in the hum of the strings, enjoying the familiar feel of the bow in his hands. For the first time since he and Zoe had seen the lavender dragon in the woods, he felt fully at peace. He was so focused, so in the zone, that he almost didn't see the exploding ball of fire right outside his window.

Flame Post and Fire Portals

Lance was so startled by the fireball outside his window, he dropped his violin.

And then the fireball did something strange. It knocked on his window. Once, twice, three times.

With his heart in his throat, Lance opened the window and let the fireball in. It floated right into his bedroom, like a small fiery butterfly. It was about the size of a tennis ball, and it was sparking.

Lance knew there was only one reason a floating fireball would knock on his window. The only creatures who used flame post were . . .

'Dragons,' he whispered.

A dragon had a message for him. Slowly, the

fireball began to unwind, like a ball of wool, and words appeared in the air.

Lance Lo, you are invited to . . .

As the words shone in the dark of his bedroom, Lance began to tremble with excitement. And then the next two words appeared.

Camp Claw.

Lance let out a shout, but the flame post wasn't finished.

Be ready.

The burning letters crackled, and with a snap, they rolled back into a fireball and floated towards the open window.

'Oh!' exclaimed Lance, hurrying to watch the fireball drift up into the night sky until it vanished.

He put his violin away and climbed into bed with a huge grin on his face. He was going to Camp Claw – the place where he might find his heart-bonded dragon and discover his own secret powers! He was thrilled, his heart still racing in his chest, but he was grateful and relieved too. Lance knew Camp Claw only invited a select number of kids every summer, and when Zoe's dragon had appeared in the woods earlier today, and there hadn't been a dragon for him, he'd assumed that was it for this year. But now anything was possible. Lance fell asleep smiling, and that night he dreamed of dragons.

The next morning at breakfast, Lance told his family what had happened the previous night.

Zoe squealed. 'LANCE! This means we're *both* going to Camp Claw! I wonder if my dragon knows your dragon!'

'Well,' Lance admitted, 'I don't have a dragon yet.'

'How can you go to Camp Claw without a dragon?' said his dad with a slight frown. 'Isn't that the whole point?'

Lance sighed. 'Dad! Camp Claw is for heart-bonded kids and ones who are likely to have heart bonds. The Dragon Force can sense potential. Don't you know that?'

His dad scratched his head. 'But how can they tell?'

'I don't know how it works exactly, but the Dragon Force has the ability to sense heart bonds and magic. And if I've been invited to Camp Claw, that means they think I probably have a heart bond of my own, I just haven't found my dragon yet.'

It was much more common for children to have a heart bond with a dragon as dragons trusted children more, but it wasn't impossible for an adult to form a heart bond too. There were many theories about why adult and dragon heart bonds were so rare, but the prevailing one was that adults had hearts that were hardened, for good or bad, and children had hearts that were open and easier for a dragon to bond with. There had been cases of dragons with dark hearts seeking out adults who had evil in their hearts too, so whenever an adult and a dragon did heart-bond, they were highly scrutinized to make sure it was in the best interests of the New World, and not just for their own personal gain.

Of course, not every human-dragon heart bond could be recorded and tracked down. Even by the Dragon Force. The true number of heart bonds in the New World was unknown.

There were stories about humans desperate for a heart bond going to Dracordia. Surviving on the new dragon-dominated continent as a human was hard, and even getting there was notoriously dangerous and difficult. You couldn't arrive by boat or plane. The only way was through a portal or dragon flight, and that meant finding a dragon willing to take you there.

The opportunity to go to Camp Claw was one of the only safe ways to visit Dracordia, and the only people allowed there were the Dragon Force themselves and Camp Claw recruits. And Lance was going to be one of those lucky people.

He grinned up at his dad. 'I might not know how it works, but the flame post told me to be ready. So I'm ready!'

'Are you sure it really happened, sweetie?' said his mum. 'It sounds a lot like a dream to me.'

'Mum, I wasn't dreaming! Haven't you heard of flame post?' Lance took another big spoonful of cereal. His appetite was back in full force. He was so excited about the flame post that he wasn't even annoyed his mum didn't completely believe him. He knew it wasn't a dream, and that was what mattered.

His mum took a sip of her tea. 'I can't say that I

have. But then it's impossible to keep up with all the new technology these days.'

Lance scoffed. 'It isn't technology. It's how dragons communicate with humans they don't know!'

'I've heard of it,' said his dad. 'I've seen it on the news. And Allison down the road received flame post from a dragon who wanted to move into her back garden. The dragon didn't want to frighten her, so it sent flame post first!'

'Well, that's nice,' said his mum. 'Very thoughtful. You hear these stories about dragons storming into people's homes, so it's lovely to hear some are more considerate. How is Allison anyway? I haven't seen her since that dragon moved in!'

'Why are we talking about Allison?' said Lance. 'Both me and Zoe have been invited to Camp Claw! This is the most exciting thing to ever happen!'

'Well, I have to say, I haven't seen any hard proof of either of your invitations,' said his dad. 'I've only heard stories about a purple dragon appearing in the woods and flame post showing up in the middle of the night. And I really think I need some more information—'

He was cut off by a thundering *boom*, and a swirling blue fireball appeared in the centre of the kitchen.

Lance's mum let out a scream. 'What is that?' she cried, a bit breathless. 'Is it flame post?'

'I don't think so.' Lance held his mum's shaking hand to reassure her. 'The flame post I received was much smaller than this one, and it was orange . . .'

Before he could say anything else, the blue fireball started to spin, expanding wider and wider until the spinning flames turned into an oval that stretched from floor to ceiling.

'It's a portal!' Zoe yelled, jumping out of her chair, excitement radiating from her like rays of sunshine. 'It's a portal to Dragon's Claw! Mum, Dad, it's happening – we're really going to Camp Claw!' She dashed towards the spinning blue flames. 'Lance, let's jump in!'

'Whoa, whoa, whoa,' said their dad, but he was smiling as he held Zoe back by the shoulders. 'Let's just wait and see what happens before we go diving headlong into a magic fireball.'

A large transparent sphere emerged slowly from the flames.

Lance's mum tightened her grip on her son's hand. 'Are we sure we're not being robbed by some sort of magical beast? I've heard that can happen, you know!'

'Don't worry, Mum,' Zoe said, stepping between her and the portal. 'I'm heart-bonded now and basically already on the Dragon Force. I'll keep us safe.'

Lance laughed, but he was glad that Zoe *did* have a dragon she could call on if this was something more nefarious after all.

The sphere continued to float into the Lo family's kitchen until it was no longer inside the fiery portal. It was transparent and completely seamless, as if someone had blown a huge liquid bubble and turned it to glass. Inside the sphere was a floating armchair.

The sphere moved further in front of the portal and stopped.

Everyone in the room stared at the strange floating apparatus that had burst into their home without invitation. Lance suddenly knew in his gut that this was *it*. This was how the adventure he'd been waiting and hoping for was going to begin. With a giant floating orb in the middle of his kitchen. He felt a strange urge to laugh. It was all so surreal, almost as if he was in a dream, but he knew it was real. His brain was trying to comprehend what his heart knew. He was going to Camp Claw, and he was going right now. He'd never felt more excited, but he was nervous too. He knew once he climbed into the sphere, there would be no turning back.

'What are we supposed to do?' whispered Lance's mum.

Zoe craned her neck back and forth, trying to look around the sphere. 'Is there a door to get inside?'

'It doesn't look as if it has a door,' said Lance. 'Maybe you just step into it?'

'Nobody is getting inside that thing until I have more information,' said their dad firmly.

Without warning, another *boom* rang out from the portal, and a second sphere emerged, settling next to the first.

Lance's dad took a step towards the floating spheres and crossed his arms. 'All right, you strange floating bubbles, explain yourselves.'

Lance glanced at his dad incredulously. 'Dad, don't be ridic—'

He was interrupted by a deep, soothing voice that flowed out from one of the spheres. 'Greetings, Lo family. Lance and Zoe Lo's transport to Camp Claw has arrived.'

Zoe let out a squeak. 'The bubbles talk! I knew this was our way to Dragon's Claw!'

'Please say your farewells and prepare to leave,' said the talking orb. 'You do not need to bring anything with you to Camp Claw except the clothes you are wearing. Everything else will be provided. The travel orbs depart in five minutes.'

'That isn't very much time,' said Lance, jamming another spoonful of cereal into his mouth. It suddenly seemed very important that he ate enough breakfast. And what did the orb mean when it said they didn't need to bring anything? What about his phone? His dragon notebook? His pyjamas? His *underwear*?

'You're leaving now?' Lance's mum sounded as if she might burst into tears.

'The flame post did say to be ready,' said Lance, but his palms were sweaty, and he was suddenly feeling more anxious than excited. Everything was happening so fast. There was so much he didn't know.

He glanced over at Zoe, who was still beaming at the orbs. At least they would be going together.

'How do we know this is legitimate?' said his dad, frowning at the orb.

'This is *clearly* dragon magic!' said Zoe. 'And it knew our names! Of course it's legitimate!'

A vaguely familiar scent filled the air, and suddenly Zoe's dragon burst out of the portal, its head filling up what little space they had left in the room while the rest of its body remained inside the portal.

'Hello, Lo family,' the dragon said. 'I sensed some anxiety through my bond with Zoe, so I have come to reassure you all.'

Zoe reached out to stroke her dragon's head. 'I'm so happy to see you again!'

'There's a purple dragon in my kitchen,' whispered Lance's mum, eyes wide with shock. 'And it's going to take my babies away!'

'Mum, we aren't babies!' said Lance, feeling his cheeks flame. He didn't want Zoe's dragon to think they weren't ready for Camp Claw.

'I will not be taking your children anywhere. The orbs will. And there is no safer place than

Camp Claw,' said Zoe's dragon. 'You must trust your children. They are our future after all.' The dragon turned to Zoe. 'I will see you there. The orbs will explain what happens next. But do hurry; they will not wait for ever.' And with a whoosh, she disappeared back into the portal.

'Wow,' said their dad, eyebrows raised. 'That was . . . something.'

'Dad, you're going to let us go to Camp Claw, right?' said Zoe. 'You've met my dragon now!'

'I don't know if that made me feel more or less reassured,' said their dad. 'But that dragon did say something smart.'

'Everything dragons say is smart,' said Lance. 'They're the most intelligent creatures in the New World.'

'Well, this one said something true. It said that you kids are the future, and you know what? It's right about that.' He sighed. 'As much as it terrifies me, I'm not going to keep you two from this opportunity. So give me and your mum a hug and then go to dragon camp. Be good, stay safe, stay together, and try to contact us as much as you can.'

Their dad opened his arms for a hug, and both Lance and Zoe squeezed him tight before turning to their mum, who was already crying.

'Mum, it's only three weeks!' said Lance. 'We'll be fine!'

'But what if something happens?' His mum blew her nose on a tea towel.

'You heard my dragon,' said Zoe, and Lance didn't miss the pride in her voice. 'There's nowhere safer than Camp Claw.'

'You know, people with heart bonds have more opportunities,' said Lance.

It was true – humans with heart bonds not only had their very own dragon, which was exceptionally useful in the New World, but it often awakened their own powers. Lance's ultimate dream was to join the Dragon Force, but if he wasn't able to do that, if he had a heart bond of his own, he'd still be able to help change the world for the better.

His mum let out a long, shaky breath. 'Oh, of course I'm not going to stop you. But promise me you'll come home safe and sound. I love you both more than you know.'

'Love you too, Mum,' said Lance as he and Zoe hugged her goodbye.

'And look after each other!' she added. 'At least you're going together.'

Lance and Zoe pulled back from their mum, who immediately turned to quietly cry into their dad's shoulder.

'So what do we do now?' asked Zoe, staring at the orbs.

'Well, they seem to talk, so maybe they can hear us too?' Lance walked up to one of the orbs and cleared his throat. 'Travel orbs, how do we get to Camp Claw?'

To Lance's delight, the orb responded. 'Your heart is the key. Place one hand on your chest and the other on one of the orbs.'

As Lance put his hand on his chest, he could feel his heart hammering beneath his ribs. He took a deep breath and placed his other hand on the orb's smooth surface. At first, nothing happened. Then he felt a warmth in his chest, and the orb began to glow. There was a crisp *click* and it split in half, opening up vertically like a set of lift doors, the floating armchair lowering to the ground as if welcoming him.

'Come and sit,' said the orb. With a gulp, Lance stepped up to the green chair and sat down gingerly. As soon as he did, the chair lifted back into the air and the two sides of the orb closed around him with another *click*.

He looked up and saw that Zoe was inside her orb too, sitting on a blue chair. She grinned at him and gave him a thumbs up, and he returned the gesture, glad to see she was safely inside.

Lance realized then how quiet it was. He couldn't hear a thing except his own breathing. He balled up his fists and tried not to think about how much trust he was putting into a floating orb that had just appeared in his kitchen. He knew that the Dragon Force had the most advanced technology in the New World, but this was way more impressive than anything he'd imagined. And more intimidating.

A melody cut through the silence, interrupting his thoughts.

Lance smiled. 'I know this tune,' he said. 'Bach's *Cello Suite No. 1*.'

'I can sense the music in your heart, Lance,' came the same deep and soothing voice from inside the orb. 'Your heart rate was elevating, and I determined it was likely this song would calm your nerves before our journey to Dragon's Claw.'

Lance cleared his throat. 'Er ... thank you ... travel orb.'

'My pleasure. Are you ready?'

Lance swallowed. Was he ready? Ever since he'd found out that dragons were real five years ago, bonding with a dragon and joining the Dragon Force was what he'd wanted most. He dreamed of soaring through the air on the back of his heart-bonded dragon.

'Are you ready to journey to Dragon's Claw?' the voice repeated.

Lance looked over to his parents, who were holding each other and smiling back at him. He gave them a final reassuring nod. 'Yes. I'm ready.'

A seat belt fastened itself around Lance's waist and over each shoulder as the orb moved towards the portal, stopping just in front of it. He glanced over his shoulder and saw Zoe gesturing and laughing inside her orb.

'Hold on – it might get a bit bumpy,' said the orb.

As Lance gripped the sides of the armchair, the orb shot through the fiery portal.

A maelstrom of colours swirled past him, first red, then orange, yellow, green and blue, as if he were passing through the colours of the rainbow, going faster and faster until they all blurred together. Lance didn't know what travelling at light speed was like, but he imagined it would feel similar to this.

Then, as suddenly as they'd entered the portal, they popped out into a large auditorium. The ceiling was made from glass and sunlight flooded the room.

Boom. Boom. Boom.

More travel orbs like Lance's appeared from their own fiery portals in the auditorium. There was a *boom* next to him and Zoe's orb appeared directly to his right, her eyes wide with wonder. Lance waved.

'*Wow*,' she mouthed back.

Soon, there were forty or so orbs hovering along the walls of the room, and a Chinese teenage girl with long black hair pulled into two braids strode onto a stage in the centre of the auditorium.

'Welcome to Camp Claw,' she said, her voice

playing inside Lance's orb. 'I'm Ling-Fei, the camp director. I'm in charge of welcoming all the new recruits. We're so happy to have you here. Now, listen carefully, because there's a lot to tell you.'

Dragon's Claw

Lance sat up straighter in his floating armchair, eager to hear everything.

'Here at Dragon's Claw, there are two missions,' Ling-Fei explained. 'The first is to keep the New World safe. That's the primary purpose of the Dragon Force.'

Lifelike holograms of dragons and their heart-bonded riders appeared above the stage. Lance recognized the signature Dragon Force super-suits with an emblem of Dragon's Claw on the chest.

He felt chills dance along his spine. Not the bad kind, like when something awful happens, but the kind that came from witnessing something amazing.

He felt the same way when he heard an incredible piece of music. And even though they were only holograms, seeing the twenty-four core members of the Dragon Force made him realize how real this all was. He couldn't believe he was actually in Dragon's Claw. He was going to be living in the same place as the Dragon Force for the next three weeks, with the chance he'd be invited to join the Dragon Force one day too.

'As you all know, humans and dragons are still learning to live together,' said Ling-Fei. 'Sometimes peacefully, sometimes not. And, of course, since the Great Collapse of the Dragon Realm into the Human Realm, other strange creatures have been appearing and causing havoc.'

The Dragon Force holograms flickered and changed to show a giant bear with lobster claws knocking over a burning building. Then it flickered again, and Lance saw the Dragon Force battling the giant clawed bear and saving bystanders from the wreckage.

'The need for the Dragon Force is greater than ever, and it's our duty to keep all beings here in the New World safe.' Ling-Fei cleared her throat and shrugged as if shaking off the terrible creature displayed above her. 'But it isn't all doom and chaos.' Her serious expression softened to a smile. 'Dragon Claw's second mission is to preserve the ancient human-dragon heart bond and use it for good. Before the Great Collapse, the bond was instant and deep, and both human and dragon gained their powers immediately. Now, the bond is more fragile, because the magical properties that enable a heart bond, and the golden elixir that powers it, have changed fundamentally.'

Lance had heard of this magical golden elixir. It had existed in the In-Between, another mythical place that humans had only recently learned of. When the Dragon Realm had come crashing into the Human Realm, the world discovered a secret place between the two realms – the In-Between. It had been explained as if the Human Realm and the Dragon Realm were two pages of a book glued together. The In-Between had been the magical layer of glue holding them in place.

The Dragon Realm's collapse into the Human

Realm was still a mystery, but there was a theory that holes between the realms had been created, weakening the In-Between. When the In-Between began to disappear, so too did the golden elixir that had once flowed throughout it. Dragons had explained the golden elixir was the source of magic and magical objects, and that anyone who obtained it, human or dragon, could become powerful.

Supposedly traces of golden elixir had leaked into the air during the Great Collapse, but there wasn't a known source of concentrated elixir in the New World as there had been in the In-Between. Lance sometimes thought this was for the best, because who knew what would happen if such a powerful substance fell into the wrong hands – or wrong claws?

But this meant that the magic source that dragons had depended on for as long as they could remember was gone. And while dragons still had their own internal source of power, it meant that certain things, like the human-dragon heart bond, had changed in strength.

Ling-Fei carried on explaining how they'd figured

out another way to build and strengthen heart bonds. 'It's something that needs to be nurtured and grown. It needs both human and dragon working together. And the period immediately following a new bond is the most critical. There's a small window in which the full potential of the heart bond can be reached. After this window, growth is much more difficult. That's why, at Camp Claw, we find those with new bonds, or those who we suspect will soon have a bond, and we help you strengthen it with your dragon.'

Lance couldn't hold back his smile. He loved imagining what his dragon might be like, what their power could be and what power it would open up in him.

Ling-Fei continued talking. 'When the heart bond is at its strongest, you may be able to supercharge each other's powers. However, the only beings we know of that have this ability are part of the Dragon Force.'

A new holographic image appeared: a mixed-race Chinese-white teenage boy with swooshy black hair on a majestic blue dragon. Lance's smile grew even wider. He knew who it was before Ling-Fei had said it out loud.

'This is Billy Chan and Spark. They lead the Dragon Force. They live here in Dragon's Claw, but most of the time they're out in the field, helping to protect the New World from attacks. When they're here though, they make sure to drop by the classes. They love to meet the new recruits.'

Lance knew that Billy Chan, along with Ling-Fei and four other kids, had been the first humans known to have heart bonds, and they had been on the news all the time during the Great Collapse. Lance had been seven back then, but he remembered it well, particularly how scared he'd felt the first time he'd seen a dragon. But through it all, Billy and the other heart-bonded humans had promised the world dragons were safe and could be trusted, and they could even be friendly, if you knew how to bond with them. That was when the Dragon Force had been born. Lance really hoped he'd get the chance to meet Billy while he was at Camp Claw. More than that, he wanted to be just like him one day. Billy was a real-life superhero, and that was what Lance wanted to be.

Ling-Fei gave the new recruits a warm smile. 'I'm here to help you discover more about yourself. With my dragon, Xing, I specialize in finding hearts that match, so if you haven't come to Camp Claw with a pre-existing heart bond, which will be most of you, we'll try to assist you in finding your dragon. We also help the heart-bonded humans and dragons to build a strong foundation so they can both grow to their full potentials. Camp Claw will last three weeks, after which you'll return home to help protect your local communities. Your dragon will either stay here and travel to you via portal when needed, or decide to move close to where their heart-bonded human lives.' Ling-Fei's eyes crinkled as she let out a small laugh. 'Even if you think the area you live in wouldn't be especially comfortable for a dragon, you'd be surprised at how good they are at making homes for themselves no matter the location.'

In the last five years, the Dragon Force had grown large enough for every major city in the New World to have its own unit on the ground. They dealt with small skirmishes between humans and dragons – like the situation between Lance, Zoe and the sleeping rock dragon – and non-threatening intruders. The core elite Dragon Force team was based in Dragon's Claw but travelled around to deal with bigger problems. They used dragon magic and high-tech systems to track unusual disturbances, and with the use of portals, the Dragon Force could be almost anywhere in an instant.

Lance knew that the Dragon Force only invited those to join the core team who were especially gifted with their powers, and had an exceptionally strong heart bond.

And of course it was only the humans who needed to prove they had what it took to be part of the Dragon Force. Any dragon who wanted to join the Dragon Force was welcome – the more dragons who wanted to help humans, the better. Then Ling-Fei said something that made Lance sit up and pay attention. 'Now, not everyone who we've invited to Camp Claw will find their heart-bonded dragon during the three weeks. The New World is large, and we don't have every dragon here.'

Lance felt his stomach clench. What if he didn't meet his heart-bonded dragon here after all?

'But don't worry – we've sensed all your hearts are open and ready for a bond. It's just a matter of finding the right dragon. It might take days, or even years, but there will always be a place for you here in Dragon's Claw, even without a heart bond.'

Lance desperately hoped he'd be one of the lucky ones to find his heart-bonded dragon while here.

'Now it's time to show you Dragon's Claw, where you'll be living for the next three weeks. Although a select few who show true potential will stay here and become part of the core Dragon Force.'

That was what Lance wanted most of all – not only to find his heart-bonded dragon, but to be part of the elite core Dragon Force living in Dragon's Claw and riding his dragon alongside Billy Chan and his other heroes.

A hologram of Dragon's Claw appeared above Ling-Fei. 'Dragon's Claw is made up of four claws, with three lagoons between them. If you hold up four fingers, each finger represents one of the four land-based claws, and the space between your fingers represents the lagoons. The majority of camp activities take place in the Palm, aptly named as it's located in the palm of the claw. That's where we are now. The Palm has two main sections – Camp Claw and the Tower, which is where the Dragon Force is based. In the Tower, we use a mix of technology and dragon magic and monitor the New World in order to detect disturbances and danger. This is an example of the work you can do for the Dragon Force that doesn't require a dragon.'

Lance bit back a groan. He didn't want to be stuck behind a fancy computer, no matter how high-tech it was. He wanted to be on the back of a dragon, saving the world!

The hologram of Dragon's Claw zoomed in. 'Now we'll take a quick look at each of the claws and lagoons in more detail, starting with the one where you'll be spending most of your time. The largest claw on the end, what you might refer to as the thumb, is the Volcano. Yes, it's a real volcano, but don't worry, it isn't active.' Ling-Fei gave a reassuring grin. 'There *is* lava in the Volcano's core, which is where some of the dragons like to spend their time, and there are rivers of lava throughout it that we suggest you stay away from, but it won't erupt.

Carved inside the Volcano are your sleep pods, as well as everything you need to feel comfortable and at home. The pods look identical, but you'll only be able to enter the one that's meant for you. Like many things at Camp Claw, the Volcano mixes the natural environment with super-technology. Here you'll also find communal bathrooms, a common room and a canteen that will provide food twenty-four hours a day, just in case you're after a midnight snack!' Ling-Fei opened her arms wide. 'Much of what we do here at Camp Claw is based on our knowledge of our recruits before we even meet them. Dragons, and by extension dragon magic and technology, can sense who you are. How do you think we found all of you?'

Lance felt another twinge of excitement in his stomach. If the director of Camp Claw was saying he was meant to be here, it really must be true.

'Now, to reach your pods, you can access them outside via orb or you can take the paths and lifts inside the Volcano itself. Next to the Volcano is the first lagoon, which you'll have noticed is a bright turquoise. This is the Water Jungle, full of lush vegetation and all kinds of miraculous water creatures. Our medics find plants to use for healing here, and our chefs forage for food for humans and dragons alike. It's also where you'll do most of your sea training if you have a water dragon. The waters here are warm and clear, and safe for you to swim in.

'The second claw is the Labs, and you'll see it glowing neon at all hours. This is where we develop our advanced Dragon Force technology, including the very orbs you're in right now! If you have an aptitude for science or molecule magic, you'll likely spend most of your time here, alongside the lab dragons.' Ling-Fei said. As many dragons like to remind us, their brains are far more advanced than human brains, so they're very useful in the Labs!' She let out a small laugh. 'Xing, my own dragon, loves to remind all humans that dragons are superior to them in every way.' She lowered her voice to a whisper. 'But even the most advanced dragons need a human heart bond to achieve their true potential.'

She glanced back to the hologram above her. 'Now, where were we? Ah, yes, the Labs. Next to the Labs is the Deep Dark. This shadowy lagoon is off limits unless you're with a trained member of the Dragon Force. The water here is, as you might imagine from the name, extremely deep, very dark and full of mysterious and dangerous creatures. We don't even know how deep it goes or what's at the bottom. Imagine swimming in ink and shadows. Of course, it's less dangerous for dragons as they have more powerful senses than humans and can see and detect things we can't. Some of our water dragons like to sleep in the Deep Dark, especially the larger ones. You might see Neptune, one of the core Dragon Force dragons, there in the mornings, practising her sound blasts.'

Lance grinned. He'd seen Neptune on the news. She was a giant sea dragon with the power of sonic blast. He was excited to hopefully meet the mammoth dragon.

'On the other side of the Deep Dark, the third claw, is the Wild Wood. This is an area of dense forest, full of trees of all kinds, as well as woodland plants and animals. You're allowed to go into the Wild Wood, but take care, as it's easy to get lost.'

Ling-Fei's face suddenly took on a solemn

expression. 'This next part is *very* important. The final lagoon, next to the Wild Wood, is the Mirage. The Mirage is made of more cloud than water, and it's absolutely off-limits to everyone. It's an area where your mind will play tricks on you, where reality bends and shifts. Even the Dragon Force, including the dragons in Dragon's Claw, avoid the Mirage. We can save you from almost anything here, but if you're lost in the Mirage, you may never be found.'

Lance shuddered. It sounded terrible. He definitely planned to stay far away from the Mirage.

'And the last claw is the Glacier. You're not forbidden from going there, but it isn't very pleasant! It's barren and cold and wind tornados run wild. Ice dragons and other snow creatures like to spend their time there. It's also where the Dragon Force trains for extreme weather.'

Ling-Fei clapped once, and the hologram disappeared. She grinned widely at the recruits in the orbs.

'Now that you know the lay of the land, how about you go and experience Dragon's Claw for yourself? To the Volcano!' Everyone in the orbs cheered wildly, and even though Lance couldn't hear them, he could see them clapping and whooping with joy. He wondered who the other recruits were and where they were from. Did any of them already have a dragon heart bond, like Zoe?

The glass roof of the auditorium opened up. 'Xing, let's ride!' Ling- Fei cried as she dashed to the edge of the stage and leaped off.

Lance saw a blur of silver swoop in from the open ceiling, and before Ling-Fei touched the ground, she was sitting on a magnificent, shimmering dragon. The long silver dragon had a serpentine face, small, elegant horns, long whiskers and scales that fanned out from her neck and behind her ears.

'Recruits, meet my dragon, Xing! And be sure to stay on her good side. Orbs, follow me!'

Ling-Fei shot out of the auditorium, and the orbs all drifted to the top, following her out over Dragon's Claw.

The Volcano

Lance was so excited to finally see Dragon's Claw that he felt as if he could hardly breathe. As his orb floated out of the auditorium, he got a bird's-eye view of Dragon's Claw. On the Palm, several large buildings surrounded the auditorium, all with clear, retractable roofs, presumably for dragons to enter and exit.

'The buildings below us are the main training grounds in Dragon's Claw,' said Ling-Fei, her voice still playing inside Lance's orb. 'The largest one is the Arena, which has been reinforced with special materials so it's almost indestructible, making it the perfect place for battle lessons and practising your powers should you bond with a dragon here. There is also the Great Hall, where there is another canteen and smaller rooms for group or individual study.'

Lance spotted a tall, modern-looking building with the Dragon Force emblem glowing at the top. He guessed this was the Dragon Force's control tower. He wondered if Billy Chan was in there right now.

'Right, I think you've all probably heard enough from me,' continued Ling-Fei. 'We'll make the short journey to the Volcano, and that's where I'll leave you to explore your new home and settle in.'

The orbs floated towards the thumb of Dragon's Claw, as riders on dragons overhead dipped effortlessly in and out of the clouds. Lance grinned at them, thrilled to be seeing more members of the Dragon Force. He could barely contain his excitement as they touched down on a beach that wrapped all the way round the Volcano. It was about the length of two football pitches from the base of the thumb to the tip.

With a crisp *click*, Lance's orb popped open, and the armchair pushed him out and onto the sand, which sparkled brilliantly white in the warm sunlight. Lance breathed in the fresh sea air and listened to the soothing sound of the waves lapping the shore. The sea was a dazzling turquoise, and at the base of the Volcano, a chain of palm trees swayed in the wind. It was like paradise and felt too good to be true, as if somehow a mistake had been made and he wasn't meant to be here. Could they cancel his invitation? Surely that never happened. He told himself to relax, instead imagining spending all his days here as part of the core Dragon Force.

All around him, the rest of the orbs landed, and the new recruits exited their pods and gazed at the beach and the Volcano with wonder.

'Enjoy the Volcano, recruits!' said Ling-Fei, waving from Xing's back. 'You'll find that security is very advanced here. Entry to all our rooms and buildings is protected by force-field technology developed in our very own Labs, but those who are authorized, and of course that includes all the new recruits, can walk right through. You have the day to explore and eat, and tonight we'll meet on the beach for the Welcome Celebration.' With another smile, Ling-Fei and Xing shot off into the clouds.

Lance's orb closed and floated back into the air. 'Wait!' he said, jumping a little to try to catch it. 'Where are you going? What if I need you?'

'You have arrived,' said the orb in its soothing mechanical voice. 'Orbs are not designed for permanent personal use. If you require an orb to travel in Dragon's Claw, you may use any that are available. Just hold one hand to your heart, and the other up in the air, and a free orb should be with you within moments. Of course, if you have a heart bond, then you are welcome to fly with your dragon instead.' The orb drifted up towards the Volcano, and Lance watched as it landed on a small rocky ledge, almost as if it was parking.

'Lance! Isn't this *amazing*?' Zoe was racing over to him through the sand, a huge smile on her face. 'I've never seen *anything* so cool! It's even better than I thought it would be!'

Lance grinned back at his sister. 'It's pretty cool.' One of their favourite things to do on their walks home from school was to imagine what being at Camp Claw was like. The Dragon Force didn't share details about Camp Claw with the general public, but, of course, sometimes rumours circulated, especially from kids who'd attended and then went home bursting with excitement about their experiences. But there were no photos, no videos and no maps. Whenever Lance had seen Billy Chan or the other members of the Dragon Force on the news, they were out saving people. Only those invited as recruits and the members of the Dragon Force knew exactly what it looked like.

Lance and Zoe had always talked about how one day they'd hopefully both get to go to Camp Claw, but they'd never imagined being there at the same time. Yet now, because Zoe had heart-bonded with her dragon, she'd been invited at just ten years old.

'Come on,' Lance said to his sister. 'Let's go and find our rooms in the Volcano.'

From the outside, the Volcano looked as Lance had expected, except for the rows of balconies and windows that dotted the upper parts of the structure. He reminded himself that it wouldn't erupt, but even so, he felt some trepidation as he and Zoe walked closer.

It was enormous, with a black craggy exterior,

and as they drew near, Lance noticed that the entire Volcano seemed to be humming, almost as if it was alive.

'Do you hear that?' he asked. 'The humming?'

Zoe laughed. 'Lance, you're always hearing music even when there isn't any!'

'No, but I really do hear something,' he insisted.

Zoe shrugged. 'Maybe the Volcano is singing. Anything can happen here in Dragon's Claw after all!'

Lance listened again, intently, and as he looked back up at the Volcano, he thought he saw a pair of eyes peering at him from the rockface. Then the humming stopped, and the eyes disappeared. He rubbed his own eyes and decided all the excitement of the morning must have got to him.

At the very base of the Volcano were three jagged cracks, big enough for a large dragon to walk through. Each of the cracks was filled with white crackling light.

'This must be one of the force fields that Ling-Fei was talking about,' said Lance when they drew close to one.

He hesitated, but Zoe skipped ahead. As she walked into the flickering white light, there was a loud beep, and she passed through as if it were nothing.

Lance quickly followed his sister inside the Volcano.

'Lance Lo,' a voice said as he stepped in. 'Dragon unknown and bond unconfirmed.'

He frowned at the assessment, but as he looked up, he was completely distracted.

The interior of the Volcano was covered in shining crystal gemstones. Sunlight streamed down from the Volcano opening, and light ricocheted and danced off the walls. It was beautiful. Dotted along the edge of the walls were tunnels, and Lance saw high-tech glass lifts zooming up and down, taking humans to their pods. In the very centre of the Volcano was a pool of crystal-clear water, steam rising out of it. Lance remembered with a jolt that lava flowed deep below.

A small red dragon, about the size of a large owl, suddenly flew out of the pool, startling a tall white girl with blonde hair, who had been peering into the water. She laughed, and so did the dragon. Then it noticed Lance staring.

'Looking for your pod? Use one of the lifts,' the feathered red dragon said.

Lance and Zoe stepped into one of the glass lifts, and by now, Lance wasn't surprised when it spoke to him. Clearly Dragon's Claw technology was so advanced it was able to recognize everyone.

'Lance Lo, Level Five. Zoe Lo, Level Four.'

The siblings exchanged a look. 'Why aren't we on the same level?' said Lance. He wanted his sister to be close so he could keep an eye on her and make sure she was safe.

'Your pod is higher than mine,' said Zoe. 'That means you're going to have a better view!'

'I'm sure the views are great from all the pods,' said Lance, rolling his eyes.

'Level Four,' announced the lift.

'Didn't Ling-Fei say there was a common room in the Volcano?' said Zoe. 'I'll meet you there in ten minutes. And then I want to find my dragon!'

With a cheery wave, Lance's little sister skipped out of the glass lift and hurried down the long stone hallway, pausing at the first pod she came to. The pods were carved into the side of the Volcano, like little personal caves. Lance couldn't see what Zoe saw, but the first pod must not have granted her access, because she kept going. He put his hand out to stop the lift from closing so he could make sure she found her pod. A moment later, the third one Zoe tried glowed in welcome. Lance smiled and gave her a thumbs up, and she stepped inside.

Whatever technology they had running through the Volcano was *seriously* impressive. Lance knew that huge strides in tech had been made since dragons had fallen into the Human Realm, bringing with them their knowledge and their magic, but he'd never seen it on display quite like this.

The lift carried on climbing up to the next floor, and Lance stepped out, marvelling all over again at the incredible design of the Volcano. The interior was a mix of natural rock, glass and steel. He took a deep breath and stopped at the first pod, feeling a little silly and self-conscious.

'Er, hello? Is this one mine?'

The pod flashed red.

'Ah, okay. Sorry for bothering you!'

As he spoke, Lance was suddenly very grateful

there was nobody around to hear him apologizing to a rock wall. It was only the eighth pod that glowed in welcome, and the stone door slid open.

'Yes!' he said with a fist pump.

'Welcome, Lance Lo,' said a robotic voice as he stepped in, and his grin grew even wider. A grey suit lay folded on the bed, and not just any suit, but one he recognized from TV. A real Dragon Force super-suit made from specially crafted fabric enhanced with dragon magic to protect the wearer against almost any kind of attack. They were shock-proof, fire resistant, could withstand freezing temperatures and even protect the wearer from the bites of all kinds of ferocious creatures. It had the Dragon Force logo on the chest and lay next to a pair of pyjamas also with the Dragon Force logo, and a few sets of underwear.

He wandered into the private en-suite bathroom and saw a toothbrush and towel. It was like staying at the best hotel ever!

But suddenly, he froze. Lance had the unsettling feeling that he wasn't alone. Something didn't feel right.

'Hello?' he said. There was no answer, but then he heard a slight scuffle from behind the shower curtain.

He gulped. Bracing himself, he whipped back the shower curtain.

A boy dressed in all black stood behind the curtain, staring back at him.

New Friends

Lance stumbled backwards, tripping over the toilet.

'Why are you in my bathroom?' he blurted out.

The white blond boy in black scowled at him. 'You're in *my* room.' He said it with so much confidence that for a moment Lance believed him. But then he remembered the pod technology meant only the correct occupant of the room could access it.

'What? No, I'm not! That's impossible. I walked in and the room *literally* said, "Welcome, Lance Lo."' Lance raised his eyebrows. 'Unless your name is also Lance Lo?'

'I suppose there's been some sort of mistake,' said the boy with a shrug.

'But the Dragon Force doesn't make mistakes,' spluttered Lance. 'This is the most high-tech magical place I've ever been!'

The boy rolled his eyes. 'Everyone makes mistakes, even dragons.' Now that Lance wasn't feeling so shocked, he realized that the boy spoke with an American accent.

'If you really thought this was your room, why were you hiding in the shower?' Lance stood firm.

'I heard someone come in and was startled, that's all. But if you're so sure this one's yours, then I guess I need to look elsewhere,' the boy replied haughtily.

'Do you want me to help you find your room?' said Lance, trying his best to be friendly despite the strange circumstances. 'What's your name, anyway?'

'I'm Arthur. Arthur Royden.'

Lance's eyes widened. 'Royden, like Royden Enterprises? The computer company? The one that makes hover boards?'

Arthur sighed heavily. 'Yes, that's the one.'

No wonder he was less impressed with the tech at Camp Claw than Lance. Royden Enterprises didn't have dragon magic, but it was one of the most advanced technology companies in the New World. Everyone wanted a Roy-Book laptop, and they made the best video games played on their high-tech console, the Roy-Toy. Lance had been asking for a Roy-Toy for years, but his parents had always said it was too expensive.

As Arthur stepped out of the bathroom, Lance noticed he wore a watch that looked like an adult's, with a black leather strap and a gold face, and he was holding a small black remote.

'What's that? Is it a new Roy-Toy remote?' he said, trying to get a better look at the object.

Arthur quickly slipped the remote into his back pocket. 'No. This . . .' He paused for a moment. 'This measures my nutrients and that kind of thing. It's to check my health.'

'Wow,' said Lance. Then something occurred to him. 'I didn't think we could bring any of our own items in here.'

'This isn't a silly phone or toy,' said Arthur scathingly. 'I need it.'

'Oh, do you have diabetes?' Lance's cousin had

diabetes and had to monitor his sugar intake very carefully and give himself regular insulin shots.

'Something like that,' Arthur said. 'But it's not any of your business so just forget about it.'

Lance was taken aback by Arthur's rudeness. 'You're the one who was sneaking around in my bathroom!' he retorted. 'How am I meant to forget about that?'

'Yeah, I suppose you're right.' Arthur sighed. 'Sorry about that. I'll go and find my own room now, and I guess I'll see you around.' With a curt nod, he quickly left Lance's pod.

'See you later,' Lance called out after him. *That was weird*, he thought to himself. Then he glanced at the clock on the wall and realized he was late meeting Zoe in the common room. He wondered if he was meant to put on the Dragon Force super-suit now, but he decided to wait. He didn't want to be the only one wearing it.

Luckily, the common room was easy to find. The map in his room showed it was at the very top of the Volcano. As the Volcano had a hollow centre with an open roof which dragons flew in and out of, and hot springs at the base, the human living spaces were arranged like a stack of doughnuts. The pods carved into the Volcano wrapped round the whole perimeter and spiralled upwards, and at the very top in the highest doughnut ring was the common room. Lance took the lift to the top floor, and as he walked into the common room, he saw the walls were made of rough volcanic stone. There were even waterfalls flowing down them, and instead of a roof there was a giant bubble dome at the top that looked as if it could close over the opening like a lid.

He glanced around the room, smiling when he spotted Zoe. She had already changed into her super-suit and was sitting on one of the sofas talking to a girl with light brown skin and brown curly hair. She had red square-framed glasses and was also dressed in her super-suit. Lance looked down at his jeans and T-shirt and wished he'd changed too.

Even from the doorway, Lance could hear Zoe talking. She didn't always realize quite how loud she was when she was excited, and Lance knew she'd never been as excited about anything as much as she was about having a dragon heart bond. Not that he blamed her.

'And then a gust of wind blew me up onto my dragon's back!' Zoe used her hands to demonstrate.

'Wow!' said the girl in the red glasses. 'That's amazing!' She had a soft lilting accent Lance didn't recognize. It wasn't American like the boy he'd just met; it was more musical than that.

'I know,' said Zoe proudly. 'I think my dragon is the most impressive of all the dragons.' Lance smiled and shook his head. Coming from anyone else, it would have sounded like bragging, but because Zoe was younger than the other Camp Claw recruits, it was hard to not be as excited by her dragon as she was. Zoe spotted Lance and waved him over.

'This is my brother, Lance! He was with me when my dragon appeared.'

Lance nodded. 'Yep. It was awesome.'

'Incredible!' said the new girl. 'And did your dragon arrive after that?'

Lance glanced down at his shoes. 'Er ... no. I haven't met my dragon yet.' He felt as if he was already lagging behind, which he knew was silly, but he couldn't help it.

The girl gave him a kind smile. 'That's okay. Most of us here haven't met our dragons yet either. I think you have to be very lucky to meet your dragon the way your sister did!'

'Yep, Zoe is pretty lucky,' said Lance with a sigh. It was true – his sister attracted luck. Good things always seemed to happen to her. And he really was happy for her, but sometimes it seemed as if she didn't even need to try. Her dragon had appeared out of the blue after all.

'My dad says I'm lucky because I was born on the eighth of August – and everyone knows that's a lucky birthday! And guess what time I was born at? Eight past eight in the morning!'

The girl laughed. 'That's a lot of eights! I didn't know eight was a lucky number. I thought it was seven.'

'Eight is the luckiest number in Chinese culture,' Lance explained.

'I guess that means my house is lucky because it's number eight on the road!' the girl replied. 'Aren't superstitions funny? In Argentina, where I'm from, people say that if you wear a red thread round your wrist it will bring you good luck.' She held out her arm, showing off a woven red bracelet. 'And even though I think it's silly, I still wear one. Might as well, you know? I'm Bea, by the way! Bea Garcia. And I live in Buenos Aries.' She grinned.

That was why her accent sounded unfamiliar – Lance had never met anyone from Argentina. He smiled back at her.

'Well, you're here at Camp Claw, aren't you? So maybe your red bracelet did bring you luck! Has Buenos Aries changed a lot?' Lance asked. 'Since the dragons came, I mean.' Most of the major cities around the world had rapidly evolved due to their new scaly citizens. Some places, like New New York and New London, had changed so much that they'd added 'New' to their names.

'I'm actually from a small town outside of Buenos Aries, which nobody else has ever heard of,' Bea said. 'But Buenos Aries has changed! There are new islands off the coast and floating above the city too! And it's popular with the dragons because it's by the sea.'

'What about your actual hometown? Has it changed?' Zoe questioned.

Bea laughed. 'My hometown is dragon-obsessed. My mama calls it Drago-Loco! Everyone there loves dragons. We keep waiting for them to arrive, to bless our town with their good luck, but so far there haven't been any. When my flame post arrived, the whole town was so excited. My papa rang the church bell, and everyone came out to celebrate that night, even though it was late. We had empanadas, and there was music, and then we all danced until dawn. I was so tired when my travel orb arrived because I'd hardly had any sleep!' Bea yawned. 'But I don't want to nap and miss anything here.'

Lance imagined an entire town celebrating dragons. It sounded amazing.

'What kind of music?' he asked eagerly.

'Guitar mostly, and drums.' Bea hummed a little tune to give Lance an idea of what it sounded like, and he began to tap his foot to the rhythm.

'Lance plays the guitar,' said Zoe proudly. 'And the violin and piano too. He's like a music genius.'

Lance laughed a little self-consciously. 'Not really. I just like music.'

Bea grinned. 'Did you see there's a guitar over there behind that sofa? Will you play something?'

'Maybe later,' said Lance, but he had no intention of playing. He loved music, it was true, but he hated performing. Whenever he had to, he focused more on the audience than the music itself, and the anxiety he felt at the thought of messing up made it hard to enjoy playing. What he liked most of all was playing by himself and getting lost in the music.

'I hope we get to see more dragons up close soon,' said Bea, glancing out of one of the big glass windows built into the volcanic wall. In the distance three dragons soared in loops, and one was blowing fire at the other, who was using their ice power to halt the flames. It was amazing to watch.

'Of course we're going to see more dragons!' said Zoe with a small laugh. 'This is Camp Claw!'

Suddenly, a loud *clang* rang out, and they all jumped. 'Is that the alarm?' said Bea. 'The one that calls the Dragon Force when they need to save someone?'

As the bell clanged again, a light laugh followed. The red owl-sized dragon Lance had seen earlier flew up from the bottom of the Volcano and appeared in the centre of the common room. 'That, dear small humans, is not the Dragon Force alarm. That is the lunch bell.'

Violent Violet

The small red dragon ushered Lance, Zoe and Bea into one of the glass lifts. To Lance's amazement, the dragon then shrank down smaller and flew in with them.

It scowled at Lance. 'It is rude to stare!'

Lance blushed. 'Sorry. I've never seen a size-changing dragon before!'

'Well, I have never seen a human boy who stares quite so much,' said the red dragon, thwacking Lance on the head with a wing. Lance winced and rubbed his head. 'Now, let me explain how mealtimes work. Food for humans is always available here at the Volcano or in the Palm. But when you hear the bell clang, that means the official meals are about to be served. You can either go down to the beach surrounding the Volcano or you can go to the Palm to collect and eat your food.'

'Thank you,' said Zoe. 'Also, your feathers are very nice.'

'Yes, I know,' the red dragon preened.

'Shall we go to the Palm for lunch?' said Lance, eager to see more of Camp Claw.

'A fine idea,' said the small red dragon. They had reached the bottom of the Volcano now and they stepped out of the lift. 'I would normally fly, and I can grow large enough to carry all of you.' Lance and Bea exchanged excited looks at the thought of their first real dragon ride. 'But I think it is useful for me to show you how to use the tunnels that run below Dragon's Claw.'

The dragon saw their disappointed expressions and laughed. 'Do not worry, small humans. You will all be able to ride dragons while you are here. But we are not a personal transport service, so you need to know how to get around without a dragon.

'The human inability to fly, combined with

the regular need to eat and sleep, is extremely inconvenient,' the red dragon went on. 'When Camp Claw was first built, a lot of time and energy was spent on solving those particular issues.'

Lance raised his eyebrows. 'What about dragons? When do they eat?'

The dragon gave a sharp smile. 'Whenever we like.'

Lance gulped. 'And sleep?'

The dragon snorted. 'Dragons rarely need sleep. If we do sleep, it is to dream.'

'I didn't know dragons dreamed,' said Zoe, her voice filled with wonder.

The red dragon glanced at her. 'There is much you do not know about dragons, small human.'

The group followed the red dragon into the centre of the Volcano and down a winding corridor that sloped deeper into the earth.

'What about the lava?' said Bea. 'Should we be worried about running into it down here?'

'The lava source is far deeper than this,' the dragon explained. 'The hot springs that flow through the Volcano, and throughout Dragon's Claw, are contained in their own channels. And, of course, we made sure the tunnels that run beneath the ground do not come into contact with the lava or any of the hot springs. Now, in you go!'

They had reached the end of the corridor, and in front of them was a round box that looked almost like a spaceship. 'You can walk through the tunnels, but that would take human legs far too long,' said the red dragon. 'So we built these tunnel crafts for humans to quickly get around Camp Claw.'

'Like the Tube in London,' said Lance as they got inside. It was long and narrow, with a few benches on the side, as well as poles for riders to hang onto.

'Humans always love to make that comparison,' said the dragon. 'I think you will find this is very different from underground trains or a subway.' The red dragon ushered them all in with its wings. 'I am staying here to make sure the other recruits know how to get to lunch, but I am sure I will see you later. Perhaps at the Welcome Celebration this evening. There will be someone at the Palm to greet you.'

With a *whoosh*, the tunnel craft shot off, moving so quickly that Lance nearly fell over. A nervous laugh escaped him. 'Whoa. This isn't anything like the Tube after all.'

A moment later, the tunnel craft came to a screeching stop, and they all climbed out. Unlike the Volcano, where the entrance was underground, the exit in the Palm was above ground and they blinked in the sunshine. Lance, Zoe and Bea stood a moment, taking in everything. Even though they'd seen the Palm on the hologram map Ling-Fei had shown them, it was amazing to be here now, in the heart of Dragon's Claw. From here they could see all the claws and lagoons, as well as the Tower that housed the Dragon Force headquarters.

'Where's lunch?' Bea whispered.

Someone walked over with a wide smile. Lance recognized him as Jordan, a Black English boy who was one of the original Dragon Force members. 'New recruits! Welcome! I'm Jordan, and this is my dragon, Midnight.' He nodded at a dark blue dragon about the size of a horse who was flying behind him, and Zoe and Bea both let out squeals.

'Midnight! You're my favourite in the Dragon Force!' said Zoe.

She flew up into the air and twirled around. 'Jordan, did you hear that? I'm the favourite! Woohoo!'

'All right, show off. Come back down!' Jordan called back with a laugh. Then he turned to the group, still smiling. 'You aren't supposed to have favourites.'

'Well, I do! Midnight has the coolest powers. And, Jordan, can't you teleport?' said Zoe, eyes wide with awe.

Jordan's grin grew. 'Wow, you know your Dragon Force facts!'

'Of course I do!' said Zoe. 'It's always been my dream to go to Camp Claw!'

'That's what we like to hear! We're happy to have you here. Now I bet you're all hungry. There's a buffet in that building over there.' Jordan pointed at a small square building next to the welcome auditorium and the training facilities. 'There's food from around the world, so whatever you like, you'll be able to find. We eat outdoors as much as we can to accommodate our dragon friends. You'll find picnic tables right behind the building. Enjoy lunch!' Jordan whistled long and loud. 'Come on, Midnight!' In the blink of an eye, Jordan was on her back.

'Teleporting is so cool,' said Zoe. 'I wonder what my power will be!'

Lance hadn't let himself properly imagine what his power might be, because he didn't want to jinx it. What if he didn't get a dragon heart bond at all and therefore never developed a power? He reminded himself that there was a reason he'd been invited to Camp Claw – that Ling-Fei and Xing had sensed something in him. He just hoped it didn't have anything to do with looking after his little sister.

The canteen was bustling with new recruits, as well as full-time members of the Dragon Force team and other Camp Claw staff.

'Jordan wasn't kidding – look at all the different types of food they have!' said Bea. 'I'm getting pizza!'

There was food from cuisines from all over the world – pizza, pasta, dim sum, dumplings, burgers, tacos, curries, stir fries, mezze, kabobs, all sorts of different salads and more. After filling his tray with all his favourites (pepperoni pizza, shrimp-fried rice and a burger), Lance headed out to the picnic tables behind the canteen.

Zoe and Bea joined him, and other new recruits

soon filled the rest of the tables. Lance guessed there were about fifty of them, all about his age. Zoe was definitely the youngest.

As Lance began to eat his burger, a familiar figure appeared. Arthur Royden was alone, holding his tray and glancing around at the tables, looking slightly anxious. Lance stood and waved, half-expecting Arthur to ignore him, but he quickly wandered over. They may not have got off to the best start, but Lance didn't want him to feel left out.

'Am I okay to sit here?' Arthur asked.

'No problem,' said Lance with a smile. 'This is my sister, Zoe, and this is Bea. We just met her earlier in the common room.'

'Hi, I'm Arthur,' he said before sitting down and inspecting his spaghetti and meatballs with such focus that Lance wondered what he could possibly be thinking. 'Do you think dragons made the food?'

Lance laughed. 'Do dragons cook?'

'I hope a dragon made this pizza,' said Bea, giggling.

'I'd rather eat food prepared by humans,' said Arthur, still staring down at his food. 'It's more hygienic.'

'Dragons are very clean,' said Zoe indignantly. 'Even cleaner than humans!'

Lance thought Arthur was being a little odd about his spaghetti, but then he remembered Arthur's gadget that measured his nutrients. Maybe that was why he was bothered about his food. 'Are you going to use your cool nutrition remote?' asked Lance eagerly, curious to see how it worked.

'I told you to forget about that,' Arthur said stiffly.

Lance suddenly realized Arthur might feel embarrassed about needing to use a nutrition remote, and he felt bad for mentioning it in front of Zoe and Bea.

'Sorry,' he said, and he meant it. He turned to the girls, trying to think of something to change the subject. 'Bea, do you have any siblings?'

'I have four brothers!' said Bea. 'Two older and two younger! I'm right in the middle.' She began to list the names of her brothers, and as she did, a shadow passed overhead.

A familiar shadow.

'Hello, human,' said a soft voice. Zoe's

lavender-coloured dragon flew in a circle above them, before landing right beside the table.

A hush settled over the picnic tables as all the new recruits turned their attention to the dragon and her heart-bonded human.

'Dragon!' cried Zoe, leaping off the bench and wrapping her arms round the shimmering lavender dragon. Zoe's grey super-suit began to shift, changing to purple right before their eyes.

'That's impressive tech,' said Arthur, almost grudgingly.

The lavender dragon glanced up at the other recruits. 'If your heart bond is true, the dragon magic in the super-suit will recognize the colour of your dragon and change to match, as Zoe's has now.'

'I love it!' said Zoe. 'It's beautiful, just like you!'

Her dragon laughed and fluttered her long, gauzy wings. 'Thank you, Zoe.'

'But you need a name,' said Zoe, crossing her arms and assessing her dragon. She took a deep breath, clearly thinking hard. 'I know! Violet!'

At the sound of the name, the lavender dragon's eyes glowed, and her scales rippled. She began to grow larger and her wings started to expand. 'Violet,' she repeated. 'It is perfect.'

'*Violent* is a better name for a dragon, if you ask me,' muttered Arthur.

Lance frowned, not understanding Lance's sudden rudeness. 'That's a weird thing to say.'

'It is indeed, but it is not wrong,' said Violet. She winked at Arthur. 'Do not forget, dragons have excellent hearing. Especially when something is said about us! But take heed, children – dragons can indeed be violent. The dragons at Camp Claw welcome you here, but do not be fooled by our warmth and hospitality. Not every dragon takes kindly to humans. And while we have the Dragon Force to help manage dragon-human relations, and to protect the New World from our shared enemies, dragons are more powerful than any other creature. So perhaps I am a *violent* Violet.' She bared her teeth and flapped her wings, purple smoke seeping out from her scales.

'Well, I've named you Violet, not Violent,' said Zoe stubbornly. 'And it suits you perfectly.'

Violet laughed. 'So it does.' She turned her gaze

back to Arthur and the rest of the group. 'Know this, new recruits. I have the power to heal, but also the power to put you all to sleep, to daze and confuse you, to stun.' Violet narrowed her eyes. 'So be careful what you say, and remember, dragons are to be respected. I am new to Camp Claw, a wild dragon who has been seeking my human heart bond. The connection I felt towards Zoe pulled me from my forest home high in the mountains to the city of London. Now we are here, and I am happy, but I have not been trained to deal with difficult humans like the rest of the Dragon Force. They see humans every day and know how to be patient with them. I am not patient.' She nodded at Arthur. 'You especially should watch your tongue. I sense that you think you are better than others here. I can tell you have a lot of human money because you smell of it, but here that does not matter. Only your heart matters to dragons. Take care to remember that.'

Lance glanced at Arthur, who had now turned very pale and almost looked as if he might pass out.

Violet gently head-butted Zoe. 'Shall we go for a flight, Zoe? To test our bond?'

'Oh, yes!' said Zoe, clapping before clambering onto Violet's back.

'Wait!' said Lance, staggering forward.

'A dragon does not wait,' said Violet. 'But I remember you. Your care and concern for your sister is sweet but not needed. There is no safer place for Zoe than with her dragon. I will protect her with every ounce of my power.'

'But . . .' Lance trailed off.

'I'll be fine, Lance,' said Zoe. She seemed older all of a sudden, and it felt strange that she was the one reassuring him, not the other way around. 'This is why we're here! You'll understand when you get your dragon.'

Lance swallowed his next words. Zoe was right.

'Flying on my back is the least dangerous thing your sister will learn to do here at Camp Claw,' said Violet. 'You must trust her. She was called here for a reason. You all were.'

'But when will you be back?' said Lance in a small voice.

'Before the welcome event tonight.' Violet looked over her shoulder at Zoe. 'Now let us fly.'

With his heart in his throat, Lance watched his sister take flight on the back of her dragon.

The Welcome Celebration

Violet was true to her word and returned with Zoe several hours later, dropping her off at Lance's pod in the Volcano.

Zoe was windswept and rosy-cheeked and beaming from ear to ear.

'Flying is the best thing ever! Lance, you're going to love it!'

Lance offered her a weak smile. 'It sounds awesome,' he said, not wanting to show how envious he was. 'Come on, we should get going. Everyone else has already gone down to the beach for the Welcome Celebration.'

*

As soon as Lance stepped out into the night, now dressed in his super-suit, the warm tropical air embraced him like a hug. Once they were past the cover of the palm trees, he could see the beach was lit with hundreds of floating flames, and he could hear the sweet twang of a ukulele accompanied by the steady beat of a deep drum. Lance felt buoyed. He loved live music. There was an electricity in the air he couldn't explain but could feel in his bones. He knew this night was going to be special.

As they walked towards the music, small sparks of light swirled around them, circling several times before shooting down towards the water, guiding their way and urging them to join in the party.

Zoe elbowed Lance in the side. 'Can you believe this? I feel as if I'm dreaming.' She lunged at one of the sparkling lights circling her. 'And what even are these little things?' Her eyes grew wide. 'Maybe they're magic dragon sprites that guide us around camp at night!'

Lance smiled at his sister. 'I don't know, Zoe, but I think we should be careful before we touch anything . . .' His voice trailed off as Zoe lunged towards another one.

'Ah-ha! Gotcha!'

Zzzzzaapp!

Zoe let out a small yowl. 'Oh, no, you don't, little sprite. You aren't getting away that easily.' She brought her cupped hands to her face and slowly peeked in. But to Lance's surprise, when Zoe opened her hands, nothing was there.

She frowned. 'Maybe it wasn't a dragon sprite after all.'

'Or maybe you just weren't quick enough,' Lance teased.

'I'll show you quick,' she said as she ran towards the beach party. 'Come on, slowpoke!'

Lance shook his head and ran after her. He was happy to have his sister with him at Camp Claw. It would have been strange to discover this place and the Dragon Force without her, having shared so many dragon encounters over the years. And there was no way he was going to let her see the Welcome Celebration before he did.

When the two of them arrived, their chests were heaving and their legs were burning from the sprint through the sand. But as soon as they paused to catch their breath, Lance immediately felt recovered, as if by magic.

'Whoa,' said Zoe, swaying a little on her feet. 'I'm not tired at all any more!' The siblings exchanged a confused look.

'There must be something in the air,' Lance said. He tilted his head to the side. 'Or maybe it's the music.'

He looked towards the source of the sound and laughed when he saw it wasn't a traditional drum being played, but a large green dragon with small wings tapping its paws on its belly. And it wasn't just any dragon. He pointed it out to Zoe. 'Look, it's Buttons! And Dylan O'Donnell!'

Lance and Zoe had seen the pair on TV many times before, two of the leaders of the Dragon Force.

'I'm pretty sure Buttons is a healer dragon,' Lance went on. 'I bet that music is why we suddenly felt so refreshed and relaxed.' He nodded along to the beat.

'The Dragon Force really has thought of everything,' said Zoe, eyes wide.

'I know!' chimed a voice behind them. Lance looked over and saw Bea hurrying over. 'One of the dragons even enchanted my glasses so they don't fall off my face!' She shook her head dramatically from side to side, her dark brown curls dancing around her face. 'See, they stay on!'

'I could happily live here for ever,' said Zoe, sighing wistfully. 'I wish Camp Claw was longer than three weeks!'

'Well, with any luck, we'll be coming back as members of the Dragon Force,' said Bea with a wide grin.

And then, without warning, the flames on the beach went out and the music stopped.

'Welcome to Camp Claw!' bellowed a charming voice with an Irish accent. 'For those of you who don't know me, I'm Dylan O'Donnell, and this is my dragon, Buttons!' The green dragon waved at them. 'Buttons and I are part of the core Dragon Force team, and I'm one of the instructors at the camp. Tonight is a special night – your first as a recruit, and the last night before your official training begins. As Ling-Fei said earlier today, one of the reasons Camp Claw was set up was to bring together humans and dragons through the ancient art of heart-bonding. But to truly understand the bond and for it to reach its full potential, you must first know yourself. That's why, most of all, Camp Claw is an opportunity for discovery. It's a chance to determine your strengths and your weaknesses. To find your inner compass. To understand your motivations, your fears, your limits.' Dylan paused and flashed a smile at the enraptured audience. 'So, in this Welcome Celebration, we're going to show you what a strong human-dragon heart bond is capable of. Please sit and make yourself comfortable. First, we have a starry welcome for you from our master of ceremonies and the Camp Claw historian.'

A periwinkle-blue-coloured dragon spiralled down from the sky. It was long and slender with whiskers that looked almost as long as its body. The periwinkle dragon swooped towards the beach and circled the group before settling just above them in the sky.

'Welcome, recruits. You may call me Kronos. My role here at Camp Claw is to teach you about the hidden history of dragons.' Kronos's eyes began to glow. 'But tonight I have a show for you, so I ask you all to look to the sky, and take in the history that is there. The stars want to welcome you too.'

Lance gazed upwards, and for the first time that night, he saw the stars. Since the Great Collapse, the night sky had changed. There were more stars now, and some could even be seen in broad daylight. Lance couldn't explain it, but he often got the feeling that they were watching him. Sometimes he even imagined the stars were musical notes that could be played, each one unique, and he'd create symphonies in his head from staring at them.

As Lance thought this, a star quivered. It was only a small movement at first, but then it became more aggressive, as if it were trying to shake free from its spot in the sky. He blinked, and another star moved. Then another. And another. It looked as if a slow and invisible river were pushing its way through the sky, nudging the stars and dislodging them from their homes. It was beautiful.

'There is much to learn here at Camp Claw, and not everything is as it seems,' continued Kronos. 'My stars, join us!'

Dozens of stars started to float down towards them, moving closer and closer until they were so near they looked like twinkling moons. As the stars moved again, Lance heard a tune in the air. One that sounded vaguely familiar. It was the same melodic humming he'd heard when he'd first come upon the Volcano! He glanced around to see if anyone else could hear it, and when he looked over his shoulder, back towards the Volcano, he gasped.

Hovering by the side of the Volcano's crater, barely visible, was a small, glowing dragon the colour of amber and flame. Its shining yellow eyes stared directly at Lance, and he felt a strange tug in his chest. He wanted to go to the dragon immediately. It was trying to tell him something . . .

As he stood up, Zoe yanked him back down. 'Lance!' she whispered. 'What are you doing?'

'There's a dragon back there,' he said, pointing at the Volcano, but the amber-coloured dragon had disappeared. Lance could still hear the humming, but it was fainter now.

'There are dragons everywhere,' Zoe said. 'And Kronos is still talking! Pay attention.'

'Do you hear that sound?' Lance whispered to both Zoe and Bea, who was also staring at him curiously.

They shook their heads. 'The music stopped when Kronos started talking,' said Bea.

Lance glanced over his shoulder once more, but there was no sign of the mysterious amber dragon. He shook his head, trying to dislodge the soft, strange humming, and focused his attention back on Kronos.

'Now the stage is set,' said Kronos. 'Let us welcome the others! Meet Charlotte and her dragon, Tank, two of our battle instructors.'

'Oh, I've always wanted to meet Charlotte!' whispered Bea. 'She's my favourite member of the Dragon Force!'

A column of fire ripped through the sky, and a huge crimson dragon with a white girl sitting on its head appeared. The dragon swooped down to the sand, shaking the ground as it settled. Charlotte leaped off Tank's head, landing in a crouch before popping up to wave at everyone. She tossed her long blonde hair over her shoulder and beamed at the crowd.

'Welcome, new recruits. In battle you must be ready for anything,' thundered Tank. 'Even the unexpected. We will help guide you to discover your physical strengths and to reach your full potential.' Tank tilted his head back, and with a throaty roar, he breathed out dozens of fire rings that rose up towards the stars, one on top of the other, creating a fiery column in the sky. The top ring was so high Lance could hardly see it.

Charlotte, standing directly under the fire rings, waved to the crowd. 'Let's see how high I can jump. Supercharge me, Tank!'

The gold in Tank's eyes brightened, and red bolts of electricity swirled round Charlotte. With a grunt, she kicked off the ground and shot into the sky. Lance was so shocked his mouth fell open. Charlotte jumped with so much force it looked as if she was flying. Up and up and up she went until she was so far away Lance had to squint to see her pop out of the top of the fire column.

Everyone on the beach cheered as Tank flew through the sky, just in time for Charlotte to land back on top of his head. Lance whooped and clapped. He was so impressed with the performance that the humming and mysterious dragon disappeared from his thoughts.

Kronos spoke again, his voice echoing all around them.

'Now, turn your eyes to the sea, and welcome Lola and her dragon, Neptune! Lola is in charge of all water training for Camp Claw recruits and the Dragon Force.'

Out of the sea rose a gigantic turquoise dragon. Neptune's head was enormous, webbed flaps fanning out from her cheeks, almost like wings. Dark grey spikes ran from the top of her head all the way down her thick neck and body. She kept rising like a huge snake unfurling itself and stretching for the sky. Sitting astride Neptune's massive neck, right behind her head, was Lola, a Hawaiian-Chinese girl, grinning and waving at them all. Her long, dark hair was wet and slicked back, and she looked as if she lived in the sea and had only come up to say hello.

'How long was she in the water?' whispered Bea. 'I didn't see her go in!'

'I've heard that Lola can slow down time,' Lance whispered back. 'So she could have jumped in without any of us even realizing!'

'Wow!' Bea's voice was full of awe, matching exactly how Lance felt.

Every human in the Dragon Force had their own unique gift, but the elite squad that made up the core Dragon Force had the strongest powers of all. Not only were they the first known humans to have heart bonds, but they were also the first to gain powers, and they had the most experience and mastery of them. On top of that, their heart bonds were the most developed, which further increased their powers.

Lola's ability to control time allowed her to exist in an almost separate time dimension. Lance knew she had been present at all kinds of major global disasters and attacks, saving countless humans and dragons, but because of how her power worked, she'd never been caught on camera using her time control gift, even when news crews had been filming. She'd suddenly appear on camera, and then the attacking creature would be apprehended by her and Neptune and other members of the Dragon Force, all within the blink of an eye.

'Aloha, everyone!' Lola called out. 'It's great to meet the newest group of recruits! I look forward to showing you all the wonders of the Water Jungle. But right now, Neptune is going to demonstrate one of her legendary sound blasts, so prepare to be stunned.' Lola laughed. 'I mean that literally!'

Lance held his breath as Neptune unhinged her jaws, showing rows of sharp teeth. She let out a mighty roar so powerful he felt as if he was standing directly beneath a jet engine. As Lance tipped his head back, he realized with amazement he could *see* the sound travelling through the air in a shimmering, trembling spiral, heading straight for the Volcano. As it struck, the Volcano shuddered with the force of the blast, but stood strong.

'You might be wondering why Neptune blasted

the Volcano,' said Lola. She was right – Lance was curious. 'The reason is because Neptune has just channelled her energy into the Volcano, fortifying it. She can alter the impact and effect of her sound blasts.'

Lola grinned at them again. 'Of course, the Volcano is strong enough to withstand and absorb a sound blast like that, but if Neptune aimed it at any of you, it would blast you across Dracordia!'

'Yikes,' said Lance.

'Thank you, Lola and Neptune. That was impressive!' called Kronos as Lola leaped off Neptune and landed on the beach to sit next to Charlotte and Dylan, while Neptune sank back into the sea, her eyes peeking out of the water. 'We still have more Dragon Force members to introduce. I wonder where Jordan and Midnight are?' Kronos made a show of looking all around.

There was a bright flash of light and Jordan and Midnight appeared out of thin air, directly above Kronos. The crowd cheered wildly.

'Hey, Kronos!' cried Jordan. 'We're up here!' With another flash of light, Jordan and Midnight appeared on the beach next to the recruits. 'Or were we supposed to be here?' Jordan smiled and winked, and everyone cheered even more.

'Jordan is so cool,' said Lance. He especially liked that there was a member of the Dragon Force from London, his hometown.

Kronos shook his shaggy head good-naturedly. 'As you can all see, Jordan's power is teleportation. He leads the lessons in the Labs, where some of you will learn how to master molecule magic.'

The temperature suddenly dropped, so much so that Billy could see his breath.

'And finally, meet the leader of the Dragon Force, Billy Chan and his dragon, Spark!'

Lance heard a *whoosh* behind him as something flew over his head. It was Billy riding an ice board. He looped and barrel-rolled through the sky as if surfing huge, invisible waves.

'Whoa,' said Bea next to Lance. 'That's impressive. Do you know how he's doing that?'

'It's his signature move with Spark,' said Lance. 'Spark uses her ice magic for the board, and Billy uses his close bond with Spark to steer it.'

'Look, Spark's right behind us!' said Zoe.

Lance glanced over his shoulder and gasped. Even though he'd seen Spark so many times on TV, and as a hologram earlier, seeing her in person was breathtaking. She was a shimmery blue dragon covered in flecks of gold, with electricity crackling around her body. She had a long swan-like neck, sharp gold antlers rising from her diamond-shaped head, an electric blue mane running all the way from the top of her head to the end of her tail and huge wings, which gave her a bat-like appearance.

Billy was still zooming towards the horizon on his ice board. When he was almost out of eyesight, he flipped round and started to make his way back to the beach.

Beside Kronos, Dylan stood up and spoke to the audience as Billy raced back. 'Billy is about as fast as they come,' said Dylan. 'He also has super-human reflexes. He and Spark are a great example of what you can achieve if you perfect your heart bond.'

As Dylan spoke, six identical white dragons rose out of the water near to the shore. They were so large, only their necks and heads were visible, the rest of their bodies still hidden beneath the waves. Moving as one, they turned to face Billy and started to fire huge ice boulders out of their jaws. Someone on the beach screamed, and Lance looked over at Zoe to make sure she wasn't too scared. His sister's eyes were huge, but she was watching the show in amazement. The white dragons continued firing ice boulders, and soon there were about twenty in the sky over the sea – all of them heading towards Billy.

Dylan chuckled. 'Ah, now this is where Billy shows off just how agile he is. I have to admit, it's very impressive, even if I have seen him do this particular trick dozens of times.'

As the first of the boulders reached Billy, he leaped off his board and jumped from one ice boulder to another, moving impossibly fast. His speed meant he seemed to be in multiple places at once, making his way closer to the beach. He ducked and dodged the boulders until he was right in front of the dragons, who were still firing at him. He dived directly at one, using its head as a springboard, and landed with a somersault onto the beach, in front of the new Camp Claw recruits.

Everyone erupted in applause.

Billy waved and took a bow. 'Hello, recruits! I'm Billy Chan, leader of the Dragon Force. Welcome to Dragon's Claw. I hope that at the end of the three weeks each of you will better understand your true self and discover the dragon whose heart matches your own.'

Dylan, Charlotte, Ling-Fei, Lola and Jordan all stood next to Billy. Seeing the elite core Dragon Force right in front of him made Lance feel as if he might burst with excitement. His heroes were real, and with any luck they'd teach him how to join them. How to become one of them.

Billy slung his arms round Ling-Fei's and Dylan's shoulders, and the six heroes grinned at each other with a comfort and ease that only comes after years of friendship. 'We know exactly how you must all be feeling right now and we're here to help. After all, it wasn't so long ago that we first discovered our own dragons and heart bonds. It's amazing, but overwhelming too. The Dragon Force is here for you. The six of us are here for you.'

Billy's words filled Lance with warmth. Even if

he never found his dragon, he was at Camp Claw and had the support of the Dragon Force. That was something to be glad of.

Billy nodded towards the group of Camp Claw recruits. 'Now, before we return the stars to their homes in the sky and send you back to your pods, we have one more surprise in store.'

A Phenomenal Match

Lance couldn't imagine what would be coming next. He'd already seen more show-stopping sights in one evening than in his entire life before today.

Billy held his arms out wide. 'We wanted to put on one more show to explain the magic behind the human-dragon heart bond and the magic that lies within this very peninsula of Dragon's Claw. To make things more exciting, two of our electricity experts will be involved.'

Spark and a bright green dragon Lance didn't recognize flew up into the sky above them.

'Greetings, recruits,' bellowed the green dragon,

its voice deep and low and almost electronic, as if it had been created in a futuristic lab.

The green dragon was larger than Spark, with a powerful body shaped like a bull's, four short, muscular legs and a long, thick neck. Its head looked like a giant upside-down triangle, with enormous gold horns that curved inwards, almost but not quite touching at the top – they looked like two boomerangs facing each other. A long pale-green beard and wiry whiskers flowed down from its face. It had a line of short, sharp spikes starting on its head, between its two gold horns, that ran all the way down its back to the base of its tail, which ended in one large spike.

'You can all call me Phenom. That is the closest human approximation of my dragon-roar name. Many of you might already know that a dragon receives a new name, granted by a human, when it finds its heart bond.' Phenom bowed his large head. 'I have yet to find my heart-bonded human, so until that day, I will be known as Phenom. Yes, like phenomenal.' Phenom preened and then carried on speaking. 'I am the leader of the Labs here at Camp

Claw, and I work closely with Jordan and Midnight. Should you have an affinity for science, and what we call "molecule magic", then our paths will no doubt cross. If not, well, you shall at least enjoy the science display tonight.'

Spark and Phenom opened their giant wings and their eyes turned completely white, shining so brightly that Lance had to shield his own eyes. The whole world appeared to dim as if the two electricity dragons were sucking the power out of the earth and the sky. The stars flickered and the moon dimmed as electricity filled the sky. And then everything went black – the stars, the moon, the sky – and they were shrouded in darkness.

'Before the Great Collapse, there were two realms,' thundered Phenom. It was so dark and still it felt as if his voice was playing directly inside Lance's head. 'The Human Realm,' he continued, and a flash of blue electricity lit up the sky. An image of the world Lance once knew appeared. 'And the Dragon Realm.' A flash of green materialized, and this time Lance saw the world that had been ruled by dragons. 'But there was another place between the two realms called the

In-Between, and this contained the source of all our magic and power – golden elixir, the rarest and most precious substance in all the realms. It has had many names over time and many wars have been fought to attain it. When the fabric between the Human and the Dragon Realms was destroyed, they collapsed into one and the golden elixir was released from its confines. This has changed the bond between humans and dragons. It is now a bond that needs to be nurtured to reach its full potential, but also a bond that leads to humans discovering their own powers.'

Zoe let out a little squeal of excitement. 'I wonder when my power is going to awaken!'

Lance smiled. He too couldn't wait to see what power his sister would have.

Phenom sent out a jet of electricity that took on the shape of an oval with a small dip in the top. 'There is a reason that Dragon's Claw is so powerful: the Heart Stone, which sits in the Palm. During the Great Collapse, the last remaining essence and magic of the Dragon Realm and the golden elixir from the In-Between solidified into a stone, now known as the Heart Stone. You have already experienced some of Dragon Claw's power firsthand, both in the orbs that carried you here and in the pods. You will see it on display in the Labs, as well as in the magic of the other claws.'

'I can't wait to see the Labs,' Bea said. 'Science is my favourite subject at school.' In her excitement, she had spoken loudly instead of in a whisper.

'Who is speaking?' roared Phenom, looking around at the group of recruits.

Lance expected Bea to hide in the crowd, but instead she raised her hand. 'It was me,' she said.

'And what do you have to say, human, that is more important than what I am saying?' Phenom came closer, his green scales crackling.

Bea held her ground. 'I said I'm excited about seeing the Labs.'

'Oh, are you? And why is that, young human?'

'Because I'm good at science so I think I'll be useful there.'

'So you think you can master molecule magic?' Phenom challenged.

Bea rolled her shoulders back and met Phenom's gaze. 'I know I can.'

Lance held his breath. What was going to happen now? He had only just met Bea, but he didn't want her to get in trouble, or worse. He remembered Violet's warning that not all dragons were patient with humans.

Phenom began to glow a bright green, electricity flowing from him.

'Your test begins now!' he roared. 'Come to the front.'

Bea strode forward, while Zoe and Lance stared after her in shock.

'One cannot have a power until they have a heart bond, so tell me again why you are so confident,' said Phenom.

Bea glanced around at the audience – the members of the Dragon Force, the dragons and all the new recruits.

And then, to Lance's complete surprise, she grinned. 'Because I'm a science whiz,' she said. 'And I know I'll find my dragon during my time at Camp Claw. I can feel it. It's been growing in me ever since my flame post arrived, it grew even more when I arrived, and right now, I can tell my dragon is close.' Bea raised her hand and reached towards

Phenom, who was still crackling with electricity. 'I think you're my dragon!'

Phenom stared at her. 'A human does not claim a dragon. A dragon reads the hearts of humans and knows who matches their own.'

Bea put her hands on her hips. 'Well, I'm pretty certain you're my dragon. Trust me, I'd rather have a less grumpy one!'

There was a burst of shocked laughter from the recruits.

'It's me' said Bea, leaning in closer to Phenom. 'Can't you feel it?'

Suddenly, a huge burst of electricity erupted from Phenom's wings, placing him and Bea inside a glowing electric green circle.

Lance stood up, ready to defend his friend, but then he saw that the leaders of the Dragon Force were watching and waiting.

The electric current had made Bea's hair rise into the air so that it stuck up all round her like a halo.

'You *are* my human!' cried Phenom. A ray of golden light shot out of his chest and met Bea's glowing heart.

'I told you!' Bea beamed at him. 'Also, your name isn't Phenom, it's Neon.'

At her words, Neon's horns twirled even higher, and his scales turned an even brighter, more electric green. He had levelled up.

The audience erupted into cheers, and no one celebrated louder than Lance and Zoe.

Breakfast and Battle Class

After Bea and Neon had heart-bonded, all the recruits were buzzing with excitement. Everyone couldn't wait to see who would be next to find their dragon.

Lance had thought that the Welcome Celebration was over, but only the show portion had finished. Now it was time for the feast – a barbeque on the beach! And it wasn't just any barbecue, it was one hosted by dragons who roasted meat, fish and vegetables with their own fire. Lance especially enjoyed the corn on the cob that Midnight had prepared. And when he was sure he couldn't eat another bite, Buttons came over with chocolate cake that looked so tempting, Lance couldn't resist.

'I've recently got into baking,' said Buttons, a little bashfully. 'I hope the cake tastes good!'

Lance and the others had just dug into their giant slices of chocolate cake when Neon approached the group and asked if Bea wanted to try flying for the first time. She leaped up on the back of her dragon, abandoning her cake, and waved to her new friends as they took off into the sky.

Lance watched in awe and hoped that soon it would be him flying through the clouds with his own dragon. But when he turned back to the table, he noticed Arthur had turned pale as he watched Bea zoom through the air.

'Are you all right?' Lance asked. 'Do you need your special nutrition remote?'

'My what?' Arthur gave Lance a confused look.

'You know, the gadget you brought from home that measures your nutrients. You look as if you might be sick.'

'Oh, no, it isn't that. I suffer from motion sickness and just thinking about flying on a dragon's back like that makes me feel queasy.'

Zoe let out a giggle. 'Well, you'd better get over it or you'll never get to fly on your own dragon!'

Arthur shrugged. 'Well, you heard what Ling-Fei said when we arrived. Not everyone who comes to Camp Claw gets a heart bond. So maybe I won't ever have to face my fear of flying and falling to my death.'

Lance stared at him. 'Mate, that's gruesome.'

To his surprise, Arthur laughed. 'I suppose you're right.'

After that, Arthur loosened up a bit, telling Lance and Zoe a bit about his life in New New York. But Lance had seen how uneasy Arthur seemed around dragons, which was a strange thing for someone who had come to Camp Claw of their own accord.

The next morning at breakfast, Lance, Zoe, Bea and Arthur sat together again. Zoe and Bea were both giddy as they traded tales about flying on their dragons. Even though Bea was two years older than Zoe, the two of them already seemed to have formed a close relationship. And the fact they were some of the only new recruits to have heart bonds brought them even closer.

The breakfast buffet at Camp Claw was as decadent as yesterday's lunch buffet. There were waffles, pancakes, porridge, congee, all kinds of eggs, cereal, fresh fruit and a whole mountain of pastries to choose from. Lance was pouring syrup on his waffle when an alarm started blaring.

This alarm didn't sound anything like the mealtime bell. It was loud and insistent and accompanied by a flashing red light.

Lance looked out of the window and saw that several dragons were taking flight with Dragon Force members on their backs, including Tank and Charlotte.

'What could possibly be the reason they'd need to send Tank? He's one of the biggest Dragon Force dragons,' asked Bea, sounding a little nervous.

'I don't know,' replied Lance, anxiously watching the huge red dragon disappear through a portal. 'But it can't be good.'

The rest of breakfast was tense as everyone worried about whatever had triggered the major alarm.

*

After breakfast, Lance and the other recruits filed into the Arena. Inside there were rows and rows of staggered columns that stretched from floor to ceiling and blocked out most of the light, but Lance could still make out the sun streaming through the glass roof.

As the group made their way past the columns to the middle of the Arena, Lance saw a fearsome dragon standing in the centre. It was black with streaks of silver, and had two gigantic feathered wings that shimmered silver in the light. It was more cat-like than any dragon Lance had seen before, its body a bigger and more muscular version of a jaguar. Thick silver horns curled around the sides of its head like a ram, and it had huge round eyes that bulged out of its skull and an enormous mouth filled with exceptionally sharp teeth.

The dragon turned and stared down Lance and the rest of the group. Its eyes bulged even further, and it flashed its teeth. 'Recruits!' it roared, jumping from side to side. 'I have been waiting months for this moment!' The dragon lowered its shoulders and dashed towards the kids, baring its teeth and staring directly into Lance's soul.

Lance thought he might faint or wet his pants or both. He turned to get away, but the dragon was already upon him, its huge mouth open as if about to grab him by its jaws. But instead of taking a bite, the dragon stuck out its huge black tongue and ran it across Lance from head to toe in one fluid lick, knocking him to his feet.

The dragon continued prancing past the recruits, licking those in its path and knocking them down too, before returning to the centre of the Arena, still hopping from side to side, its tongue flapping in the air.

Lance looked at the dragon again. Its features, while still terrifying, seemed softer now, and the way it was jumping up and down made it look like an overexcited puppy.

'Eryx,' said a familiar voice from behind them, 'you said you'd control your instincts this time.'

Lance turned around to see Dylan and his dragon Buttons had followed them into the Arena.

'I am sorry, Dylan,' replied Eryx, his head down. 'You know how I get.'

Dylan chuckled as he ran past the group and gave

the dragon a pat on his muscular shoulders. 'Don't worry, Eryx. I'm sure the recruits will understand.' Dylan turned to the audience. 'Recruits, meet Eryx, your battle instructor for today.'

Eryx stood up straight and let out a ground-trembling roar so loud and deep it shook Lance's bones and his composure. The dragon shook his head as if trying to rid himself of the giddiness that had overcome him. When he looked up at the group again, he was calm.

'Hi, recruits. My sincerest apologies. As Dylan says, battle is my speciality, and my instincts are my greatest strength, but sometimes they get the better of me. I have whatever it is canines have that makes them like to be affectionate towards humans. That is why I licked some of you.' Then he let out a loud growl. 'But do not be fooled. I also have the canine instinct to hunt, and I am more dragon than anything else, so my bite is very powerful.'

Lance gulped.

'Charlotte and Tank normally lead this lesson, but they had to tend to an incident elsewhere.' Lance and Zoe exchanged a look, and Lance knew his sister was thinking the same thing he was. What was the mysterious incident?

Eryx continued, 'Now, let us begin your first lesson. We are here to learn how to battle. How to be warriors to protect those in the New World, but –' the dragon widened his eyes – 'before we learn how to battle, we must first learn how to occupy the same space as humans and dragons. We must learn how to move as one. As humans tend to say, we must learn to crawl before we walk or run.' Eryx bared his teeth and opened his wings to their full span. 'Or fly. We will need volunteers to demonstrate the basics, and who better than Zoe and Bea and their heart-bonded dragons.' Eryx motioned for the two girls to join him, and as they made their way to the centre of the Arena, Violet and Neon floated down from the sky.

Zoe let out a small yelp and leaped straight into the air towards Violet, who swooped down and caught Zoe on her back. Violet swirled around as if returning Zoe's enthusiasm. Her uneven sets of wings fluttered slowly and rhythmically as her long serpent body curled in the air. She always seemed to be moving and twisting, her wings fluttering in a way that was almost hypnotic.

'Well done, Zoe!' roared Eryx. 'Recruits, take a look at Zoe. You can see that even though she is not holding on with her hands, she has no trouble staying on Violet, which is good for Zoe as Violet is always moving. Zoe is staying in place because of the strength of the bond. Not all of you who heart-bond with a dragon will find it as effortless as Zoe. It depends how much trust there is between you and your dragon. When the trust is there, you will naturally stay on, even though there is no seat or foothold. It will be as natural as breathing; it will happen without thinking. And in fact, thinking too much about it often makes it worse.'

Lance watched his sister in awe. She already had a dragon *and* she was a natural. He hoped he'd find his own dragon soon. He looked at Eryx and wondered if he could be his dragon. Should Lance do what Bea had done last night and tell Eryx that he thought he was his dragon? Would that work? But the more he watched the powerful dragon, the more he realized that Eryx wasn't his heart-bonded dragon. Bea must have really felt her bond with Neon to claim him so confidently as hers.

Eryx gave Dylan what looked like a grin, which was a fairly terrifying sight. 'These two are exceptional. One would never guess they only bonded recently. Perhaps the two of you can do some battle training too.' Eryx turned his grin to Zoe. 'What do you say, Zoe? Are you and Violet up for some light manoeuvring?'

Zoe's eyes looked like they were about to pop out of her head. 'Of course we are!' Violet nodded in assent.

Buttons let out a cackling roar. 'Your enthusiasm is truly admirable. In case you're worried, which you're clearly not, I'm an expert healer should anything happen.'

'All right, class,' said Dylan. 'Everyone except for Zoe and Violet, please step away from the centre of the Arena until you reach the pillars. They will need space for this demonstration. And don't worry, Bea, we haven't forgotten about you and Neon. The two of you will help us with the next part of this lesson.'

Bea climbed off Neon's back and gave Zoe a thumbs up. 'Show us what you can do!'

Dylan looked at the device on his wrist and pushed a button. A holographic screen appeared in front of him with an array of virtual switches. 'Ready?' Dylan asked, his hand hovering above the device.

Zoe flipped her hair out of her face. 'Always.'

As the recruits shuffled to one side of the Arena's battleground, a strike of lightning flashed in the air. The class turned to see a ball of lightning had appeared opposite them.

'In this exercise,' Dylan continued as he made his way under a pillar, 'Zoe and Violet will practise flying and manoeuvring as one. The lightning ball you see was developed in our Labs, and as you might expect, it shoots bolts of real lightning. The goal of the exercise is simple – don't get struck.'

'Bring it on,' said Zoe, her eyes gleaming with anticipation as Lance watched on with a mix of pride and nervousness.

Dylan pressed the device on his wrist again and the screen reappeared. 'Let the training begin,' he said as he flipped a switch.

The ball of lightning sparked to life, and the

tangle of electric bolts within it whirled around as if trying to escape. There was a loud *crack* and a bolt of lightning shot directly at Zoe, but she and Violet saw it coming and dodged it effortlessly.

Zoe grinned. 'Too easy.'

The lightning ball whirred as it rose up and fired five more bolts at Zoe and Violet. Violet barrel-rolled and spun like a corkscrew in the air, dodging the attacks.

Eryx let out a grunt of approval. 'Impressive manoeuvre. The two of you are moving as one.' Eryx turned his massive head to address the class. 'Recruits, you may think that Violet is leading this, but you would be wrong. When a heart-bonded human and dragon fly together, they fly as one. Violet can, of course, control her own movements, but as the trust is there, Zoe can also control Violet through the bond, helping her dodge oncoming attacks and manoeuvre in ways that wouldn't be possible for her to do on her own. Think of it as a beautiful dance that requires phenomenal balance and precision, but instead of two dancers, there is one with two minds. To move as one, the minds must be in sync.'

Violet backflipped in the air above them. 'Is that

all you've got?' Zoe asked Eryx with a smile. Lance buried his face in his hands. Of course his sister would be goading the battle instructor. She really was fearless.

Eryx let out a low rumble. 'Let us take it up a notch.'

Dylan hesitated. 'Are you sure you're ready for more?' he asked Zoe.

'Didn't you hear me the first time?' Zoe quipped, a twinkle in her eye. 'I'm always ready.'

'Be careful, Zoe!' Lance called out. He couldn't help himself. He was her protective big brother after all.

'Don't worry,' she yelled back. 'Violet and I can handle anything.'

'Your sister sure is confident,' said Arthur.

'That's an understatement,' Lance said, shaking his head. But he was proud of Zoe for impressing the Dragon Force and the entire group of recruits.

Dylan flipped another switch on the screen and the sky above them lit up. Three more lightning balls appeared in the Arena. 'Here we go! Careful what you wish for.'

Zoe leaned forward on Violet's back, preparing herself as the lightning balls circled the two of them in the air. The balls began shooting bolts, with so many flashes of lightning that Lance had to shield his eyes.

The Strength of the Bond

Lance had never seen so much lightning before. The Arena looked as if it was putting on the epic finale of a fireworks show. But Violet and Zoe dodged each and every attack, like a trained boxer dipping and swaying to avoid being hit. The balls continued circling them, firing a torrent of lightning strikes from every angle. Violet seemed to be moving in every direction at once, her long body dancing in the air, a swirling maze of loops and whips as the lightning strikes whizzed by.

'Astonishing,' said Eryx. 'You two are quite the pair.'

Dylan tapped the switch on the holographic

screen. 'Yes, yes, very impressive. I think that's more than enough manoeuvring for today though.' He furrowed his brows. 'That's odd.' He pressed the switch again. 'My control panel has frozen.'

A brilliant flash of lightning filled the room once more, and three more lightning balls appeared, starting to fire even more bolts at Violet and Zoe.

'Can you slow them down a bit?' said Zoe, sounding breathless.

Lance sat up straight. He could tell his sister was nervous, which worried him more than anything. Nothing scared Zoe.

'Don't worry, Zoe!' said Dylan, his voice higher than usual. 'I'm just shutting it down now.' Dylan tapped the switch for a third time.

There was another flash in the Arena and three more lightning balls appeared. Once again, they started to fire. To Lance's horror, a bolt struck Violet.

Violet let out a roar of pain and whipped her head round to Dylan. 'You said this was light practice! TURN IT OFF!'

'I'm trying!' cried Dylan, his panic now apparent.

But more and more lightning bolts were shooting out of the glowing balls, getting faster and faster. Violet and Zoe kept dodging them, but Lance knew they wouldn't be able to continue for much longer.

'Do something!' he yelled. 'Eryx, can't you stop it?'

Eryx gave a low growl and leaped at one of the lightning balls, trying to bat it out of the air, but his attempt was futile.

And then one lightning bolt shot even faster towards them.

Lance yelled as he watched his sister jump off Violet. She was preparing to block her dragon from the electricity using her own body as a shield. The lightning bolt hit Zoe in the heart, and Lance fell to his knees. He felt as if he couldn't breathe, as if his vision was going dark, as if the whole world was going dark. This was his fault – he should have never let Zoe come to Camp Claw. She was too young . . .

Suddenly there was a loud cheer, and Arthur yanked Lance to his feet.

'Your daredevil sister is fine,' he said. 'Look!'

Lance looked up and gasped. Zoe was somehow on

Violet's back once again. And all around her, doing flips and blocking the bolts, were dozens of Zoes.

'She's replicated herself!' said Arthur. 'And it doesn't seem to be an illusion because the replicas are being used as shields!'

It was true. The not-Zoe Zoes were using their bodies to create walls between the lightning bolts and the real Zoe and Violet.

'This is incredible,' said Eryx.

One bolt hit a replica Zoe, and with a poof, both the replica and the lightning bolt disappeared.

'LANCE!' real Zoe suddenly shouted, and he leaped up, ready to dive towards her. 'ARE YOU SEEING THIS? I CAN MAKE MORE OF ME! HOW AWESOME IS THIS?'

'It's super awesome!' Lance yelled back as another replica Zoe exploded into dust. 'And also super weird!'

'Shut down!' said Dylan, pressing another button on the screen. Finally the glowing lightning balls disappeared, and so did the remaining Zoe replicas.

'Ah, there we go.' Dylan wiped his brow.

Violet landed on the ground, and the real Zoe swayed on her back for a moment before hopping off.

'That was quite the ... exercise,' said Violet, dipping her head and licking the deep wound in her side.

'I'll take care of that,' said Buttons, swooping down next to her. He placed his paws on Violet's wound and closed his eyes. A soft, soothing purr came from deep in his throat, and Lance saw the wound seal itself until it disappeared entirely.

'Good as new,' said Buttons.

Violet inspected her side. 'It was the least you could do after trying to kill us with lightning!'

Dylan ran over to Zoe. 'Are you all right? That wasn't supposed to happen ...'

'No kidding,' muttered Lance, his heart still racing from seeing his sister nearly get fried.

'Am I all right? Of course I am! I discovered my power, and it's *awesome*!' Zoe beamed and stroked the side of Violet's head. 'And Violet did amazingly too!'

'I'm just glad you two have such a strong bond. Things could have ended very differently otherwise,' said Dylan.

'I knew my human was talented,' said Violet smugly.

Eryx glanced at Dylan. 'Should we stop the training session there?' he said. 'I have never seen our technology go haywire like that. It might be too dangerous to continue showing the recruits.'

'Finally a dragon talking sense,' said Arthur approvingly. Lance glanced to his side and saw Arthur holding a notebook filled with notes he'd taken in the lesson. 'Who would want to go into the Arena after *that*?'

'Wait, I want to try!' called out Bea. 'I want my power to be awakened too!'

Lance fought the urge to laugh. 'That's who.' It seemed Bea and Zoe were destined to be friends.

Dylan groaned. 'Not today I'm afraid,' he said. 'I need to take my tech up to the Labs to see what the issue is.'

Bea pouted. 'Well, isn't there something else me and Neon could try that doesn't require tech?'

'My human has a point,' rumbled Neon.

'I have an idea,' said Eryx. 'You two, step into the Arena. Do not worry, Dylan, we will not do anything dangerous.'

Dylan rubbed his temples. 'Dragons have a

different definition of "dangerous". Your idea had better be safe. Billy will never forgive me if anything happens to the recruits.' He gave the crowd a crooked grin. 'Nobody's died at Camp Claw before and I'd like to keep it that way.'

'First of all, I must say, well done, Violet and Zoe. That was extremely impressive. Zoe, I have never seen that power manifested. It is an exceptional one, and it will be very useful for battle.'

Zoe beamed at the praise.

'Now, recruits, part of the reason that Zoe was able to awaken her power so quickly and so strongly is due to the strength of her heart bond with Violet. They are clearly already very trusting of one another. That is an important part of the human-dragon heart bond.' Eryx laughed a little. 'Or at least that is what I am told. I do not yet have a heart bond. But I am still one of our greatest warrior dragons.'

Arthur snorted. 'Dragons are so humble.' Lance shushed him. He couldn't understand why Arthur was being insulting.

'Now, where was I?' Eryx went on. 'Oh, yes. Can everyone please take note of how Violet's eyes are glowing, even though she isn't actively using any of her powers? This is one way to tell if a dragon has a heart bond or not. Those who have bonds always have glowing eyes. I like to think it is the warmth in the dragon's heart shining outwards. And when a bond is particularly strong, some dragons will even change physically, or to use a human term, they "level up".'

Lance remembered seeing Violet's eyes glowing when she discovered him and Zoe in the woods.

'Zoe, can you and Violet please step to the side,' Eryx said.

Lance wanted to yell out to Zoe, to tell her to sit by him so he could make sure she was okay, but he held his tongue. His sister had proven she was more than capable, and he knew Violet would look after her. It felt strange to see Zoe suddenly doing things he couldn't help her with, how she was mastering new skills he'd not learned.

Zoe glanced over her shoulder and gave her brother a big smile and a thumbs up, and he returned the gesture. 'Good job,' he mouthed, and he meant it. Then he chuckled. He couldn't wait to tell his parents his sister could now create decoy Zoes. That was certainly going to make it easier for Zoe to do her chores at home!

'Bea and Neon, please come forward,' said Eryx. 'As I said, we will not be using any of the tech, but I do have an idea to show off the power of your heart bond. Bea, I want you to look into Neon's eyes and tell him what you are thinking, but not with your words.' Eryx paused and gave the recruits a meaningful look before continuing, 'I want you to tell Neon what you are thinking with your *thoughts*.'

Bea gazed into Neon's eyes, her face scrunched up in concentration. A few moments passed and Lance could see beads of sweat forming on her brow.

'Do not force the thoughts, Bea. Let them flow,' instructed Eryx.

Bea closed her eyes and took a deep breath in before letting it out slowly. When she opened her eyes, she was calm. She gazed once more into Neon's eyes, her own eyes wider this time, almost unfocused, lost in her thoughts.

Neon blew green sparks from his nostrils. 'Well,

that is a preposterous idea for an invention. But it just might work.'

Bea gasped and stumbled backwards. 'That is so *cool*.' She peered into Neon's eyes again, and the dragon chuckled. Bea burst into laughter with him.

'You are thinking like a true Labs inventor now,' said Neon. Bea beamed at him, and then at the rest of the class.

'Success!' roared Eryx, hopping up and down. 'I can tell you are going to be an extraordinary group of recruits. It usually takes a few days for someone to confidently ride a dragon and even longer for our first successful telepathy. A strong heart bond allows a human and dragon to be able to read each other's minds. Spark and Billy were the first dragon and human duo to master this, but with the Great Collapse, the link between the mind and the heart bond has become even more intertwined, and now it is something that all heart-bonded pairings can achieve if the bond is strong enough.'

'Of course my human knows how to communicate telepathically with me,' said Neon with a grumble. 'We already have a very strong bond!'

'And my human has already found her power,' said Violet with a sniff. 'She has proven to be an excellent dragon rider with very little practice. I imagine she is the best rider Camp Claw has ever seen.'

'Well, you would not know, would you?' grumbled Neon. 'As you are new to Camp Claw and only came here because of your human.'

'Yes, because our bond is so strong, I could sense her on my own. I did not need the camp to find her. Unlike some of you,' Violet snapped back.

For a moment, the two dragons glared at each other. Zoe and Bea tried not to laugh as their dragons bickered over who had the better heart-bonded human.

Eryx cleared his throat. 'Well, class, I think that's enough for today. Does anyone have any questions?' he asked, surveying the crowd. Then he frowned. 'Hey! Boy at the back! Are you even paying attention?'

Lance realized Eryx was talking to Arthur, who had continued to scribble in his notebook.

Arthur looked up and addressed Eryx. 'As if my life depended on it,' he said flatly.

Eryx leaped across the Arena and landed next to Arthur in one swift movement. He circled him once, his leg muscles rippling under his black and silver scales, and then he licked Arthur from head to toe.

'I know you,' Eryx said. For a moment, Lance saw true fear flash across Arthur's face. Eryx sniffed Arthur audibly. 'You smell familiar to me.'

Arthur looked as if he might pass out.

'YOU ARE MY HUMAN!' roared Eryx.

'What?' said Arthur, sounding truly shocked. 'How is that possible? How do I have a heart bond with a dragon?' But as he spoke, the telltale golden charge shone out from Eryx's heart and met Arthur's own.

A smile, a real smile, stole across Arthur's face, and he gingerly reached out to pat Eryx behind his head. Eryx let out an audible purr, and the class laughed.

'I like the name Eryx,' said Arthur fondly. 'But I think I'll call you Jaws. It suits you much better.'

Jaws roared his approval.

Infinity

Lance lay awake that night in his pod, tossing and turning. He should have been tired after the busy day, but he couldn't fall asleep. Following battle class in the Arena, the recruits had been taken up to the Labs. There it had felt like stepping into the future. High-tech equipment filled the room and they had been invited to try it all out. Bea was a natural, just as she'd suspected.

After lunch in the canteen, Lola showed the group the Water Jungle. It was full of so many plants Lance had never seen or heard of, and there were thousands of rainbow-coloured fish darting around in the water. Everything there was brightly coloured and vibrant. Lance and the others hadn't swum in the Water Jungle, but Neptune had created a giant bubble that kind of looked like a travel orb for the class to stand in. It had moved around the Water Jungle like a submarine. Lola said once the recruits had a heart bond, they'd be able to swim in the water alongside their dragon and learn about the plants and marine life.

Zoe and Bea were going back to the Water Jungle tomorrow, and they'd invited Arthur to come along too. Lance had stood there while they made plans, feeling somewhat neglected because he wouldn't be able to join them. Now everyone else in his little group had heart bonds, he desperately hoped his dragon was waiting for him around the corner too.

He sighed. Playing one of his instruments always managed to soothe his nerves, and tonight his fingers felt restless, so he left his pod and headed up towards the common room where he'd seen a battered old guitar.

Phew. The guitar was still there.

Lance sat down with the instrument in his hands, and immediately felt better. It was the most relaxed he'd been all day. He was about to start playing when suddenly he heard a noise.

The humming melody from the Welcome Celebration was back, and it was louder! Lance sat and listened, trying to place the tune. Then he began to strum a new tune that layered a harmony over the humming. He let his fingers glide over the guitar, plucking the notes that felt right and letting the melody speak for itself. The notes were a language Lance understood, a language that sometimes came easier to him than words or feelings. In the dark of the common room, he let the strings reveal for him what his thoughts couldn't. What Lance loved most about music was that it was universal; something that everyone could understand and enjoy.

The sound that came from Lance's fingers answering the humming melody surprised him. It was a calling. A yearning. A reflection of his heart. Lance strummed the notes on the guitar until he felt at peace. Then he paused to let the silence wash over him. Except . . . when Lance stopped, the melody he had been strumming continued to play.

Lance shook his head, trying to remove the melody that seemed to be clinging to him. He paused and listened. The other sound, the humming, had stopped, but the melody he'd just been strumming was *still* playing. *Where is it coming from?* Lance thought.

He stood, trying to pinpoint it, and followed the sound to a small waterfall on the interior wall of the room. It sounded as if the melody was coming from inside the volcano wall. Lance ran his hand underneath the water and was surprised to find it was hollow behind the water. Without thinking twice, he walked straight under the waterfall and crossed through to the other side. Behind it was a long passage, lit by small glowing crystals similar to the ones in the main cavern of the Volcano.

Now he was through, Lance could still hear the music, echoing the melody he had played, and he followed the passageway. The air was warm, and his clothes and hair quickly dried, and soon the tunnel began to widen, growing to show a cavern.

And it wasn't empty.

Standing in the centre was a dragon Lance

recognized right away, even though he'd only seen it once before and from a distance.

'You!' he said.

It was the dragon he'd seen by the Volcano on the night of the Welcome Celebration. The one who had been staring right at him. It was staring at him again now, its huge yellow eyes wide in wonder.

Up close, Lance could see the dragon was larger than he'd thought. It wasn't huge like Tank, but it wasn't tiny either – about the size of a small horse. It had glowing amber scales that looked gold from one angle and orange from another, like dancing flames. On top of its head were four long, curved horns, almost like a crown, and at the base of each horn was a large gemstone – sapphire, emerald, ruby and diamond. It had a short, wide snout, and instead of a mane, it had a row of small, pointed orange gemstones, like spikes, running from its head all the way down its back and along its tail. The dragon was standing on its back legs, like a raptor, and was much taller than Lance. Its wings were folded in tightly against its body, but Lance could see how large its wings were, even folded.

The dragon cocked its head to the side, watching Lance with a mix of curiosity and bafflement. The music Lance had heard, the music echoing his own tune, had stopped. The only sound now was the distant rushing of the waterfall that Lance had walked through.

'You hear the humming too, Lance Lo,' said the dragon.

'Yes!' said Lance. 'I heard it when I first saw the Volcano and again when I saw you at the Welcome Celebration!'

'You heard it when the stars came close,' said the dragon solemnly. 'It is the song of the stars. Few can hear it. I have been waiting to meet someone who can hear it too.' Then the dragon gave Lance a wide toothy grin. 'I heard the music you made!' The dragon began to hum, mimicking the sound of the guitar, and Lance nodded in time with it.

'You sound just like a guitar!' he said, impressed.

The dragon let out a short laugh. 'I am good at mimicking sounds, even though it is not the most useful skill for a dragon to have.'

'I think it's a pretty cool skill,' said Lance, grinning

back at the dragon. But then all of a sudden, he began to feel anxious. What if he wasn't meant to be here? Had he accidentally intruded on the dragon? 'I didn't mean to disturb you.' Lance gazed around the small cavern. 'Do you live here?'

'Sort of. I live deep in the Volcano, but I often roam the tunnels throughout it.' The dragon bowed its head, looking bashful. 'I am not very helpful to the recruits, you see, because I lack useful skills, so I mostly stay hidden.'

'Are you part of the Dragon Force?' Lance asked. 'I've never seen you on TV.'

The dragon let out another small laugh. 'I do not go on rescue missions. I never leave Dragon's Claw.'

'Oh, right. Do you want me to leave you alone?' Lance said, feeling a little uncertain.

The dragon shook its head. 'No, Lance Lo. I called you here. I knew that you had heard the humming, and tonight I was certain you would hear it again. I have music in my heart too. I am often lonely here in the Volcano, and music keeps me company.'

Lance's own heart, also filled with music, began

to pound very hard. Could this be who he thought it was . . . ?

The dragon looked away. 'I do not fit in here at Dragon's Claw, even though it is the only home I have ever known. Everyone here is a hero, and I am meant to be one too. There was a prophecy about me being the long-awaited Infinite Dragon when I was still in an egg. But when I hatched, I was a simple dragon. My powers have not manifested as it was foretold. Perhaps they will one day – dragons live for a long time after all – but for now I feel I am of no help to anyone. That is why I stay hidden and play my music. I am too embarrassed for anyone to see me.'

'I'm sure you're an amazing dragon!' said Lance, already feeling strangely protective of this mysterious dragon.

The dragon gazed at Lance with fire in its eyes. 'I have always been curious about humans. I have known them since I was a hatchling. Billy Chan and his friends rescued me, and when I hatched, their faces were the first I saw. They have always been kind, of course, and made sure I had a home here in Dragon's Claw, but my gifts are not obvious. I cannot heal, I am not especially strong in battle, nor do I see visions of the future.' The dragon seemed to shrug. 'My scales change colour. The colour you see now is what I usually look like, but I can change them.' The dragon closed its eyes, and a moment later it was red, then green, blue, and, for a brief moment, sparkling white before it returned to burning amber.

Lance wasn't totally sure how he was meant to respond, so he applauded.

'This is a small feat for a dragon, as is mimicking sound. Parrots can do that, and chameleons can change colour. I was foretold to be the Infinite Dragon, yet these skills do not seem worthy of such a title.' The dragon looked down again. 'I grew tired of always being asked what I could do. If a new power had awakened in me. If I could sense my human heart bond. I never had an answer they liked. So I hid in the Volcano. I know Dragon's Claw better than any, and there are many places one can hide, even as a dragon.'

Lance remembered now that he had heard about

the golden dragon egg Billy Chan and Spark had saved, right before the Great Collapse. It had fallen into the In-Between, and Billy had ventured into it and battled a spidragon to save the egg. When he emerged with it, the egg needed to be protected and hidden because it was so valuable. There had been rumours of an Infinite Dragon, a dragon who would help unite humanity and dragonkind, but as far as Lance and the general public knew, no dragon had ever appeared. And it seemed everyone had forgotten about it.

But here it was: the Infinite Dragon, who'd been hiding in Dragon's Claw for the past five years.

The dragon looked at Lance, blinking its huge eyes. 'I was always told I would know when I met the human I shared a heart bond with, that it would awaken something in me. But I didn't know what that meant until yesterday, when I realized you had heard the humming, and then again tonight when I heard you playing the guitar.' The dragon gazed down at Lance. 'Mimicking music may not be very useful in battle, but it brings me happiness. And for that, I treasure it. It is hard for dragons to find happiness. It is one of the reasons we are drawn to humans, especially young humans. Joy comes to you so easily.' The dragon hummed again, swaying back and forth. 'Your music makes me happy, Lance Lo.'

Lance smiled. 'Music makes me happy too,' he said.

'I know,' said the dragon. 'Because I can see what is in your heart, and you have music there. And kindness, hope and ambition.' The dragon's eyes began to glow. 'I am ambitious too. I want to be respected by my fellow dragons. I want to be useful to the Dragon Force. I want to prove that I was worth saving as an egg.'

'Of course you were!' Lance burst out. He tentatively patted the dragon. It was a little strange, standing next to a dragon towering above him on its hind legs. The dragon could probably run on all fours as well, if it needed to, but it would be very low to the ground, like a scampering meerkat.

The dragon smiled, showing rows of small, sharp teeth. 'See? You are kind. And I think, Lance Lo, that you bring out kindness in those around you. Kindness is needed now more than ever in this time of constant battle in the New World.' The smile disappeared. 'I am not a seer dragon, but even I know the hardest time for humans and dragons is still to come. I have heard a warning in the song of the stars. They know something they cannot tell us, but they are trying to warn us that bad times are coming. There is a reason Billy Chan and his friends have worked so hard to build a strong Dragon Force. I believe his dragon, Spark, has seen something in the future. Spark knows what it is that the stars sing of, and so she and Billy know that the Dragon Force must be prepared.'

Lance shuddered.

'Billy and Spark and the rest of the Dragon Force know the truth about dragons and humans. They know we are stronger together.' The dragon's heart began to glow gold. 'And I know that you, Lance Lo, are my human. I have been waiting for you, here in the Volcano. I know you will help me unlock whatever power is in me, and I will do the same for you.' A prism of golden light beamed out of the dragon's heart and into Lance's chest, which he saw was now also glowing gold.

'I know your name,' Lance said suddenly. 'Your name is Infinity.'

'Infinity,' whispered the dragon, and then all the gemstones at the base of her horns shone even brighter until the entire cavern was full of dancing rainbow light. Suddenly, Infinity's wings flew open, and the edges grew sharper and more dangerous. The row of spiked gems along Infinity's back sharpened too.

For Lance, it felt like a puzzle piece being snapped into place. He felt a sense of wholeness. He had his dragon. Now they were heart-bonded, he could sense she was a female dragon, and that, while she claimed not to be able to do anything powerful, she could breathe fire. But there was something else too.

'Your scales don't just change colour, do they?' he said.

Infinity locked eyes with him. 'No, they can also change to gemstones, like the Diamond Clan, the dragons who protected me as an egg. The four of them were once the most powerful clan of dragons. They were forged deep in the core of a mountain, in a pool of fire, and they emerged as gemstone dragons.

They are not my parents, but they passed on the gemstone power to me. And, just like them, I enjoy spending time deep in mountains and volcanoes. It makes me feel safe.'

'Where are they now?' asked Lance gently. He could sense through his new heart bond with Infinity that there was a deep sadness in her about the Diamond Clan.

Infinity closed her eyes for a moment. 'They disappeared when I was still a hatchling. Nobody knows where they are or what happened to them, but I believe they are still out there somewhere. Perhaps one day they will return. I hope so. They were the closest thing I had to a family. I never knew my mother dragon – she died in battle and was turned into a star.' Infinity's eyes flew open. 'I believe she is one of the stars singing a warning to us. I do not know what it is though. Nobody else can hear it, and for a long time I thought I was imagining it.'

'I heard it,' said Lance. 'But it didn't sound like a warning to me; it sounded like . . . a calling.'

'And it is! The stars called to you, and when you answered, you found me.' Infinity smiled, showing her sharp teeth. 'I am glad you can hear the song of the stars, Lance Lo.'

'Me too,' said Lance. Then something occurred to him. 'If you hatched after the Great Collapse, does that mean you're less than five years old?'

Infinity laughed. 'In human years. But dragons age differently to humans. We live much longer, and we age faster. A five-year-old human, I understand, is still basically a hatchling.'

Lance nodded. 'That's true. But you shouldn't be so hard on yourself for not knowing what all your powers are. My parents are always telling me I've got my whole life to discover my true potential. You should listen to that advice too.'

'Your parents sound wise,' said Infinity.

Lance laughed. 'They're all right.' He felt a sudden pang of homesickness for his mum and dad. He couldn't wait to tell them he'd found his dragon.

'I saw your sister on the night of the Welcome Celebration,' said Infinity. 'She has her dragon too.'

'Yes, now we both do,' said Lance, cheering at the thought of flying alongside Zoe. At the thought of flying at all.

Lance cleared his throat, suddenly nervous to ask about the one thing he'd been desperate to experience. 'Can ... can we fly?' He felt as if he'd been waiting for this moment his whole life.

Infinity smiled widely. 'I am glad you asked.'

She crouched down, and Lance clambered on her back. He had been worried about sitting on the sharp spikes, but he found they flattened beneath him. He remembered what Ling-Fei had said about how the heart bond made it easy for a human to ride their dragon.

'Ready?' said Infinity.

'Yes, but where are we going?' Was Infinity about to fly him back through the passage he'd entered and into the common room?

'To explore Dragon's Claw.' Infinity turned towards the inside wall of the Volcano and roared. As if answering her call, a small hole began to open in the wall, until it was large enough for Infinity and Lance to fly through. He stared at it in amazement.

'I have never flown with a human on my back before, so I hope I know what I am doing!' said Infinity.

Lance grinned. 'Well, I've never ridden a dragon before, so we can learn together!'

'Then here we go!' sang Infinity, and she leaped into the night.

Lance couldn't help but laugh as he felt the night air rushing past him. He was flying on the back of his dragon, and it felt like the most natural thing in the world. It was completely amazing. He let out a whoop as Infinity flew higher, until they were so far above Dragon's Claw he could see the entire peninsula below – all four claws, the lagoons in between and the long arm that connected it to the Dracordia mainland. In the moonlight, he could see the different colours of the lagoons. The Water Jungle was still turquoise, but in the night it looked luminescent. The Deep Dark was an inky black with swirls of purple, and the Mirage was a swirling silver, shot through with golds and greens.

'I want to see everything!' Lance cried out, leaning over to get a better look.

Infinity laughed. 'Another night, perhaps. We should get back inside the Volcano. But I am excited to show you more of Dragon's Claw another time.'

Lance could sense that Infinity was anxious, and while he didn't know why, he wanted to make sure his dragon felt safe.

They flew around the Volcano once more and then back into the hole that Infinity had opened. As they landed gently inside the small cavern where Lance had found his dragon, the hole in the rock behind them closed up.

Lance stared at it. 'Is that dragon tech?'

Infinity glanced over her shoulder. 'Not exactly. I know how to coax things out of this place. Nobody knows Dragon's Claw as well as I do' Her eyes opened wider. 'Maybe do not tell anyone I can do that. I do not want to get in trouble!'

Lance grinned at his dragon. 'Your secret is safe with me.'

Infinity took a deep breath. 'I am nervous about being out in the open so humans and other dragons can see me. But I am proud to be your dragon, and tomorrow, with you by my side, I will be braver.'

'Don't worry, Infinity,' Lance said. 'We're in this together. You won't be alone.'

'I know,' said Infinity, eyes glowing. 'I have felt

lonely for a long time, but not any longer.' Then she jolted, as if she'd just remembered something. 'Oh, I almost forgot! I have a present for you!'

Lance laughed. 'I don't need a present when I have a dragon! That's the best present I could have asked for!'

'I think you will like this present. I found it once in the Mirage—'

'I thought Ling-Fei said even dragons don't go to the Mirage,' Lance interrupted.

Infinity wrinkled her face up with a mischievous grin. 'I know Dragon's Claw. Now, do you want the present or not?'

Lance smiled. 'I definitely want the present!'

Infinity walked to the side of the cavern and Lance noticed a pile of things. 'What's all that?' he asked, curious.

'This is my hoard! Dragons love to hoard precious items. Some hoard gems or gold. Buttons got his name because he collects buttons. I collect things I am drawn to. And when I found this item, well, I knew I needed to keep it. I had a feeling that one day, if I ever met my heart-bonded human, it would bc useful to them.' Infinity reached into the pile and withdrew a stringed instrument Lance had never seen before. She held it out, along with a bow.

The instrument looked like a sledgehammer resting on its head with two strings running from one edge of the hammer to the tip of its handle. The bow's hair was threaded between two strings.

'How do I play it?' asked Lance, carefully examining it.

'You rest the bottom of the erhu on your hip. One hand holds the bow and moves back and forth in a similar motion to playing the violin, while the other hand holds the neck. You move your fingers up and down the strings to change the pitch. Of all the human instruments that I know, the erhu is the one I feel most resembles the human voice. One can hear the emotion in its sound.'

Lance tried to position the erhu the way Infinity had explained. He glanced up at her. 'Can *you* play this?'

Infinity laughed. 'I have claws, of course, but this instrument is not meant for dragons to play. I make my own music.' She began to sing softly, and Lance found himself mesmerized by it. 'I look forward to hearing you play the erhu.'

Lance tentatively drew the bow across the strings, and the sound that came out of the erhu was rich and soulful. One moment it was low, the next it was high. He realized he was playing the same melody that had come to him in the common room, the song Infinity had echoed back. He felt tingling in his fingertips, and he wanted to keep playing, but he was worried someone might hear. Even though it was the middle of the night, the sound could carry, and he didn't want anyone to find Infinity's secret cavern.

'The erhu was meant for you,' said Infinity. 'You play it beautifully.'

Lance blushed but was pleased by the praise.

'Will I see you tomorrow?' he said.

Infinity nodded. 'I will meet you in the Palm and join you for your classes.' She dropped her gaze. 'I will admit I am nervous. Even though I know all about Camp Claw's classes, I have never attended any.' She looked truly nervous. 'I hope everything goes okay. I have a tendency to attract calamity.'

'You'll be great,' said Lance, patting his dragon on the back. '*We'll* be great.' Then he smiled at her. 'Well, goodnight, Infinity!'

'Goodnight, Lance. Oh, and one more thing before you go. Let me see if I can do this right.'

Infinity shut her eyes, and a moment later, Lance heard her voice inside his head.

If you need anything, you can always reach me down our bond.

'Can I reply?' said Lance excitedly.

Of course, said Infinity's voice in his head.

I'm really glad you're my dragon, he thought.

Infinity's reply came instantly.

Me too, Lance. Me too.

Powers Awakened

When Lance woke the next morning, he worried for a moment that last night's events had all been a dream. That he hadn't found Infinity in her secret cavern and that they hadn't heart-bonded. But then he saw his erhu leaning against the pod wall, and he realized all of it had been real.

Lance fist-pumped the air and leaped out of bed with renewed energy and excitement. Today was the first day at Camp Claw that he had a heart-bonded dragon. The first day to really prove to the Dragon Force he deserved to be here. Him and Infinity both.

*

Lance waited to tell Zoe his news until they were in the canteen having breakfast. Bea and Arthur were with them too. They'd fallen into an unspoken agreement that they would eat all their meals together and attend classes together too.

Lance noticed other Camp Claw recruits had also formed their own small groups, and he was glad he and Zoe had made friends quickly. Even though Arthur was still a little stand-offish and aloof, he was also funny and made wry observations. Lance could tell that almost despite himself, Arthur liked spending time with the group. Bea was warm, kind and laughed easily, and Lance felt as if he and Zoe had known her for years instead of days.

The four friends sat at a round table together, planning their day. Zoe, Bea and Arthur were all wearing their dragon super-suits, which had shifted colour to match their dragons' scales. Lance's suit had changed overnight from grey to the fiery orange and amber of Infinity's scales. He'd purposefully stayed in his pyjamas for breakfast so he wouldn't give away his heart bond immediately.

'We've got Ling-Fei's class first thing, which is

specifically for heart-bonded humans and dragons,' said Bea, shooting Lance an anxious look. 'So shall we meet up with you after that and we can all go to the Labs together?'

Lance saw Zoe bite her lip, and he knew his sister felt bad for him. Even Arthur, who still seemed stunned by the fact that he had a heart bond glanced down at his bowl of cereal.

'What are you going to do this morning?' Zoe asked, keeping her voice bright.

'Well,' said Lance, taking a bite of his scrambled eggs. 'I thought maybe I'd join you guys for Ling-Fei's class.'

There was a moment of awkward silence.

Arthur cleared his throat. 'Lance, I don't think you can come if you don't have a heart-bonded dragon . . .'

'Oh, that's right,' said Lance with a sigh. Then he grinned. 'Good thing I found my dragon then!'

Bea was so shocked she spat out her orange juice. 'What? How? When?'

'Lance! Are you serious?' squealed Zoe, clapping her hands.

'But ... but ... we all went back to the pods together last night!' spluttered Arthur.

Lance laughed. 'It happened after we went to bed! I couldn't sleep and then ...' He was going to tell his friends about the humming he'd heard, but he didn't want to sound weird. He knew from the Welcome Celebration that Zoe and Bea hadn't picked up on it. 'I decided to go to the common room to play the guitar, as music usually helps me relax, and when I was playing, I heard my own music echoing back to me! I followed it and found a dragon! My dragon!' Lance continued to tell them about how he and Infinity had bonded, and that she'd given him the erhu.

'I'm so happy for you!' said Zoe, leaping up out of her chair and coming to hug her brother.

'I can't wait for you to meet Infinity,' said Lance. 'But she's a little shy and nervous about seeing everyone.' He explained how she'd spent much of her life hiding, anxious about disappointing the other dragons after her prophecy hadn't come true.

'I know I'll love her!' said Zoe loyally. Then she

paused. 'Not as much as I love Violet, of course, but if she's your dragon, she must be amazing.'

'She is,' said Lance.

'You know what is cool?' said Bea thoughtfully. 'We each have our own dragons and heart bonds, but we get to know each other's dragons too! It's a whole dragon crew!'

'That's what makes the Dragon Force so special,' agreed Lance.

'I still can't believe I have a heart bond,' said Arthur, sounding genuinely shocked. 'I never thought that would happen.'

Zoe laughed. 'What did you think would happen when you came to Camp Claw?'

Arthur furrowed his brow. 'I . . . I don't know.'

'You're clearly interested in learning more about dragons,' said Lance, remembering how Arthur had been taking notes during yesterday's battle class.

Arthur dipped his head and moved his cereal around the bowl. 'Can I tell you guys a secret?'

The others nodded and leaned in closer as Arthur lowered his voice to a whisper.

'I want to learn as much about dragons as I can

because I'm afraid of them. Or at least I was.' He paused. 'Everything is different now that I, well, now that I have Jaws.'

'Afraid of dragons?' repeated Bea. 'But dragons are incredible!'

'I get it,' said Lance. He told the group the story of when he and Zoe had woken up the sleeping rock dragon. 'I thought it was going to eat me alive. And honestly, when Violet first appeared, I was afraid of her too. Dragons *are* incredible, but they can be very dangerous.'

'And not all dragons are friendly,' said Arthur, voice wobbling. Lance suddenly realized his friend was close to tears. 'You guys might already know this, but my dad died last year.'

Lance did know. It had been huge news when Peter Royden, head of Royden Enterprises, had died.

'What the news channels didn't report was what really happened.' Arthur paused. 'A rogue dragon killed my dad.'

Zoe and Bea both gasped, and Lance felt sick to his stomach.

'I'm so sorry,' he said. 'That's awful.'

Arthur blinked rapidly, still fighting back tears. 'Yeah, it was. It happened eight months ago, but sometimes it feels like yesterday.' Arthur adjusted his watch. 'This watch was his. I wear it so he's with me every day. Maybe that's a weird thing to do.'

'No, it isn't weird,' said Lance.

'After my dad was killed by a dragon, I hated all dragonkind. I thought every dragon was evil. I never thought I would bond with one. But I couldn't say no to the invitation to come here. I wanted to face my fears. Nothing prepared me for what it would be like to come to Camp Claw and bond with my own dragon though. I didn't think I could ever trust dragons and feel safe around them, but I do with Jaws.'

'What happened to your dad is terrible,' said Bea. 'But I'm glad you've realized that not all dragons are evil.'

'It was really brave of you to come to Camp Claw,' said Zoe.

'Zoe's right,' added Lance. 'I bet the dragons can sense how brave you are.'

'Do you really think they can see inside our

hearts?' Arthur asked. He sounded a little nervous, and he kept fiddling with his watch.

'Definitely!' said Zoe. 'How else would they know who has a heart that matches their own?'

'I guess you must be right,' said Arthur, but he still seemed unsettled.

'Jaws saw that his heart matched yours,' said Lance. 'You're meant to be here, Arthur.'

Arthur gave him a small smile. 'Thanks, Lance.' Then he chuckled. 'Also, dude, why are you still in your pyjamas?' Lance could tell he was trying to change the subject.

He grinned at his friends. 'Because I didn't want you guys to guess straight away that I had a heart bond now. My super-suit changed colour last night. It looks awesome. I should probably change before we all head over to Ling-Fei's class together.'

As the four friends emerged out of the tunnel craft into the Palm, Lance saw Violet, Neon and Jaws all waiting for them.

Infinity wasn't there.

'Hey, Lance,' said Zoe. 'Where's your dragon?'

'I don't know . . .' said Lance. He knew he hadn't dreamed it, but what if Infinity's nerves had got the better of her? What if, despite the bond, she was too shy to train with the other dragons? What would he do then?

Infinity? he asked down their bond. *Are you coming?*

A moment later, he heard her reply.

I am nervous, she thought back.

Me too, said Lance. *But we can do it together.* Through his mind, he sent her a calming tune he made up on the spot.

He felt her brighten.

Thank you, Lance. Hold on. I am coming!

While he'd been communicating with Infinity through their bond, his friends had walked over to their dragons. Zoe was petting Violet, Bea leaped up on Neon's back as if she'd done it hundreds of times and even Arthur climbed astride Jaws.

'Hello, Lance,' said Neon, sounding bemused. 'I see your super-suit has changed colour. I recognize that orange, but I cannot quite believe it. Is your dragon . . . ?' He trailed off as Infinity flew down from the sky, landing directly in front of Lance. She stood on her hind legs and gazed back at the other dragons. In the sun, her scales sparkled, and the four gemstones at the base of her horns shone brightly.

'This is my dragon,' said Lance proudly. 'Infinity.'

'An appropriate name,' said a voice from behind them, and Lance turned to see Billy and Spark. 'Infinity,' Billy said, grinning. 'I'm so glad you found your heart-bonded human.'

'Me too,' she replied.

'I told you that you would,' said Spark.

'Seer dragons say a lot of things,' said Infinity.

'Prophecies are not always straight forward,' admitted Spark. 'Even I do not know exactly when things will come to pass. I can only see glimpses. But I saw you happy with a human heart bond, and now here you are.'

'Congratulations, Lance,' said Billy. 'And congratulations to all four of you for finding your dragons. I'll be accompanying you this morning to your class with Ling-Fei and Xing. The heart-bond class is one of my favourites at Camp Claw. I'm usually too busy with Dragon Force duties, but this morning I've got some free time.' His grin widened.

'I can tell you four are a special group. You remind me of me and my friends when we first met and found our dragons.'

Lance felt a warm glow spread through him at Billy's words. He couldn't believe Billy Chan knew who he was and he was going to spend the morning with them.

Billy nodded towards Zoe. 'I heard about what happened yesterday. I'm so sorry I wasn't there! Spark and I were battling a three-headed shadow snake.' He shuddered. 'Nasty creature.'

'Is that what Charlotte and Tank were fighting yesterday too?' asked Bea.

Billy raised his eyebrows. 'Very observant,' he said. 'But they had their own monster to battle.' He sighed. 'I'll be honest with you, recruits. There's recently been a huge increase in attacks. The Dragon Force is doing everything it can to protect the New Earth, but it's worrying how frequent they've become.'

Lance gulped. He hoped his parents were safe in London.

'Don't worry, Billy,' said Zoe. 'You've got us now!'

Billy laughed. 'I like the enthusiasm, but you guys need training before we can send you out in the field. And on that note, let's get to Ling-Fei's class in the Wild Wood. She and Xing are already there. Follow me!'

Billy and Spark lifted up into the air, and the other four dragons followed. The group flew across the Palm, heading in the direction of the Wild Wood claw.

Isn't the Wild Wood dangerous? Lance thought to Infinity as they soared through the air.

Not to me, Infinity thought back, her tone amused. *And you will be with me, so you will be safe.*

Lance realized in that moment, with Infinity by his side, he could face anything.

The Wild Wood was beautiful. It was full of huge trees with leafy canopies that the dragons skilfully manoeuvred around to land in a large glen with high, wavy grass. Ling-Fei and Xing stood waiting, and she smiled and waved when she spotted Infinity, her eyes lighting up.

'Oh, look how much you've grown!' said Ling-Fei.

'I have a name now too,' said Infinity proudly.

'Infinity,' added Lance.

'It's perfect,' Ling-Fei replied.

'So you have decided to grace us all with your presence, little dragon,' said Xing. 'It is about time.'

Infinity ducked her head. 'I was waiting for my human.'

'Well, perhaps now we will see what the prophecy meant,' said Xing.

'Xing, be nice,' said Ling-Fei. 'I, for one, am very happy Infinity is here. Today we're going to be working on strengthening your bonds with your dragons, and hopefully awakening your powers if they haven't yet been revealed.' She grinned at Zoe. 'I hear you have a very impressive power! Do you think you can replicate yourself now, even though you're not in danger?'

Zoe squeezed her eyes shut in concentration, and suddenly four more Zoes appeared in the glen. Each one stood waiting for a command from the real Zoe. Zoe lifted up her arm, and as she did, the other Zoes lifted theirs.

'Amazing,' said Billy. 'Xing, you can sense magic

and how it works. Is Zoe turning the air into an apparition that looks like her and can even fight like her, but isn't actually an extension of herself?'

'I suspect so,' said Xing. 'There is only one way to find out. Zoe, I am going to attack one of the replicas.'

Violet let out a low growl.

'Oh, calm down,' snapped Xing. 'It is to help the child improve her gift!'

'That's okay with me,' said Zoe, and three of the replicas disappeared with a poof, leaving only one in front of Xing.

Xing lunged at it with her small, sharp claws, and the replica Zoe shimmered out of existence before popping up again behind Neon. There was no sign of injury.

'I felt resistance, but it was like sand,' said Xing. 'They will be very useful in battle. They have physical form but are not lasting.'

'Very useful indeed,' said Billy, looking impressed. 'Thank you, Zoe.'

Lance desperately hoped his power would awaken soon and that it would be something just as exciting and useful as his sister's.

'Now, as you all saw yesterday, Zoe's power awoke in the face of danger. That's a common occurrence. But sometimes all it takes to find your power is to look within yourself. The Wild Wood is rich in dragon magic, which is one of the reasons we teach classes here. Remember, stay with your dragon at all times.' Ling-Fei nodded towards Arthur. 'Arthur, why don't you and Jaws come into the centre?'

Jaws scampered forward, like a giant puppy, with Arthur close behind.

Ling-Fei spoke in a low, calm voice. 'Arthur, focus on your bond with Jaws, and how it makes you feel in your heart.'

Lance remembered what Arthur had said about his fear of dragons and hoped this exercise would make him feel at peace.

Arthur closed his eyes for a long moment, his hand on Jaws's back. Jaws stood very still, and Lance wondered if they were communicating through their bond.

Suddenly Arthur's eyes flew open. 'I know where we are,' he said.

Zoe laughed. 'Yes, we're in the Wild Wood, silly.'

Arthur shook his head. 'No, I mean I know exactly where we are. I can see it in my head like a map. I can sense where there are buildings and land and sea.'

'Interesting,' said Billy. 'How confident are you?'

'Very,' said Arthur.

'Can we test it? Safely, of course,' said Billy.

Arthur nodded, and Billy turned to Jaws. 'Jaws, drop off Arthur in the Wild Wood maze. You know the one I mean.'

'But what if he gets lost?' growled Jaws.

'I don't think he will,' said Billy. 'But if he does, you can fly back to him.' He glanced at Arthur. 'Does that sound okay?'

Arthur nodded again. 'I know where the maze is. I can see it in my mind.'

'Well, then you'll be back with us in no time,' said Billy with a smile. 'I've seen this power once before. It's a type of pathfinding map magic. It gives you the ability to sense patterns and pathways that other people can't find.'

Arthur grinned. 'I do like puzzles.'

'That makes sense,' said Billy. 'Good luck with the maze!'

Arthur leaped up onto Jaws and they disappeared into the trees. 'See you soon!' he called back. 'I know I can find my way!'

'This class has started very well!' said Ling-Fei, sounding pleased. She turned to Lance and Bea. 'Are you two ready for your powers to be awakened?'

'Yes!' cried Bea immediately.

'Lance?' said Ling-Fei, her eyes kind. 'What about you?'

Lance had never been so ready for anything in his life. 'Absolutely.'

The Wild Wood

As excited as Lance was, he decided to let Bea go first. She'd discovered her heart bond before him after all.

'Bea, you start,' he said, nodding towards the centre of the glen where Arthur had been standing when he found his power. Lance hoped Arthur would make his way back to them soon. It was one thing to be able to visualize paths and another to make your way out of a maze in a potentially dangerous wood.

'Thanks, Lance,' said Bea, clearly appreciative.

Bea and Neon walked into the centre of the clearing.

'All right, Bea,' said Ling-Fei in a soothing voice.

'Try to focus on your bond with Neon. If your power is ready to be awakened, it will respond. You'll feel it.'

Bea put her hand on one of Neon's spiralling horns. His horns began to glow a bright green, and as Lance watched, the green glow seemed to transfer to Bea, until she too was glowing. Suddenly she gasped.

'I can sense the molecules of the metal in the earth below us! I can feel Neon's electric current too! But there's something else.' Bea crouched down and put her hands on the earth before letting out a frustrated sigh. 'If I could just reach the metal, I know I could shape it. I could make something from it!'

Ling-Fei smiled. 'I can help with that.'

Lance remembered Ling-Fei's power was an affinity with nature. She could speak to trees and cajole mountains to move. He watched in awe as she put her hands above the ground and closed her eyes. Moments later, tiny particles of metal burst out of the earth until a small ball of iron had formed.

Ling-Fei opened her eyes and glanced at Bea, who was staring in amazement. 'Will this do?'

Bea nodded and held out her hand. Ling-Fei tossed her the iron ball, and Bea easily caught it. Her hair began to rise up around her, and a crackling sound filled the air.

Bea pulled on the iron ball, and it broke apart like clay. 'Perfect.' She looked at her dragon. 'Please can you give me a little bit of electricity, Neon?'

Neon's horns sparked, and a small lightning bolt flew from his horn to the pieces of iron in Bea's hands. Bea then drew her hands apart, but the iron pieces stayed floating in the air. She moved her hands quickly, as if conducting an orchestra, and the pieces of metal moved too, the bright green lightning bolt whizzing from one piece to the next.

'Molecule magic,' said Billy quietly. 'She's rearranging the molecules of the metal and creating something, using the electricity to power it.'

Bea was muttering different numbers to herself, and Lance realized her magic was linked to equations and science.

'Almost done,' said Bea, sticking her tongue out of the corner of her mouth in concentration.

A moment later, she beamed at them and held out

her hand. On it was a tiny metal replica of Neon that moved and breathed fire.

'Excellent! You clearly have a gift for molecule magic and building things,' said Billy. 'And it appears you have a link with metal and electrics. Your power means you know how things work, but more than that, you can take things apart and make them into something new.'

'Wow!' said Lance. 'That's such a cool power!'

'It's amazing!' agreed Zoe. 'Can you make me a mini metal Violet?'

Bea laughed. 'I can try!' She winked at Neon. 'I told you I'd be good at molecule magic!'

Neon let out a low chuckle. 'So you did, and you are very gifted at it. I have never seen a human with such an affinity for it. Not even Jordan, who leads the Labs.'

Bea's smile grew. 'I can't wait to check them out!'

'Well, we are heading there next,' said Neon.

'Wait!' said Lance. 'I still need to awaken my power, right?' He was suddenly a little panicked there wouldn't be time for him to try, or that his power wouldn't manifest as easily as it had for his friends.

'Don't worry, Lance,' said Ling-Fei with a warm smile. 'I haven't forgotten about you.'

'Oh, I can't wait to see what your power is!' said Zoe, clapping with excitement.

'Me too,' said Lance with a nervous laugh.

We can do this, Infinity thought down their bond.

With a deep breath, Lance walked into the centre of the glen. Infinity crouched down on all fours, making it easy for Lance to put his hand on her head, right next to the four gemstones shining at the base of her horns. He closed his eyes and waited for something amazing to happen.

'Focus on the bond,' Ling-Fei said. 'We'll start there, and if that doesn't work, we can try something else.'

Lance's eyes flew open. 'Why don't you think it will work?' he said. Ling-Fei hadn't said that to anyone else. Why was she saying it to him?

'I meant that in a reassuring way,' said Ling-Fei kindly. 'I'm sure it will work, don't worry.'

'But you can't force it,' added Billy. 'So just try to relax.'

Lance nodded and closed his eyes again. *Relax*, he told himself. *Focus on the bond.*

You feel tense, Infinity said through their bond. *Think about music — that always calms you down.*

I can't think about music, Lance said back. *That will distract me. I have to focus on our bond to reveal my power.*

After a few moments, Lance sighed. 'How do I know when my power is awakened?' He still had his eyes closed.

'You'll know,' said Billy with a surety that Lance found comforting.

'It's a feeling,' added Bea. 'I could suddenly feel the metal in the earth, all around us, and I knew I could manipulate it.'

'Mine wasn't really a feeling. I saw the whole world laid out like a map in my mind,' said Arthur.

Lance's eyes flew open. 'Arthur! You found your way back!'

His friend grinned at him. 'Yep. The maze was tough, but I could see it as if I were a bird above it so I knew where to go and how to get back here.'

'That is the fastest a recruit has ever found their way out of the Wild Wood maze,' said Jaws proudly.

Lance sighed again. 'I can't believe you found your

way out of an entire maze before I've even worked out what my power is.'

'My power appeared because I felt threatened,' said Zoe. 'And it wasn't a feeling or a thought, it just happened, like *boom*!' As she said 'boom', three replica Zoes appeared. She laughed. 'Just like that!'

'Okay,' said Lance, his stomach starting to churn with anxiety. 'So should one of the dragons blow fire at me or something?'

'I do not like that idea,' said Infinity quickly. She bowed her head. 'Perhaps I am the problem. I have not come into my full powers yet, so it makes sense that my heart-bonded human wouldn't have either.'

'No, you're not!' said Lance, wrapping his arms around Infinity and giving her a hug. 'You're my dragon. You're meant to be my dragon. My powers are just . . . blocked for some reason.'

'Watch out!' Zoe suddenly cried, and Lance looked up right as a huge clod of dirt flew at him.

'Ah!' he yelled, and the dirt hit him square in the chest.

'Thought it was worth a try,' said Arthur with a shrug.

'You threw dirt at me!' Lance exclaimed, wiping the mud off him.

'I thought your powers might awaken like Zoe's did. It looks like I was wrong,' Arthur said, sounding extremely unrepentant.

'That would not be enough to awaken a power,' said Xing. 'But perhaps this is.' And then before Lance knew what was happening, the silver dragon zoomed towards him, picking him up in her coils and lifting him high in the air.

This was *nothing* like flying with Infinity. This was terrifying. At first, Lance tried to wriggle out of her grip, but the higher she soared, the more petrified he became, and he was starting to feel like he was going to pass out. Awakening his power wasn't meant to feel like this.

'Please!' he cried. 'Put me down! I'll try harder! I'll figure it out!'

Xing ignored his pleas and soared higher and higher, and then, without warning, she dropped him.

16

Molecule Magic

Lance plummeted through the air like a stone.

He scrunched his eyes shut. 'THIS WOULD BE A REALLY GOOD TIME FOR MY POWER TO AWAKEN!' he shouted. There was no reply.

Surely the dragons wouldn't let him impale himself on a tree? Surely they'd catch him before he fell to his death?

And then Infinity was underneath him, and through the bond he landed on her back easily. Lance felt a huge sense of relief as the two of them safely flew back down to the glen.

'Lance! Are you okay?' Zoe ran over to him as he tried to catch his breath. He nodded but found he didn't trust himself to speak.

Xing joined them and raised an eyebrow, clearly unimpressed with the results.

'Xing!' Ling-Fei burst out. 'That wasn't very nice!'

'I knew his dragon would catch him,' said Xing blithely. 'And I thought perhaps it would scare his power out of him. I do not know what else we can do.'

'Sometimes it takes time,' said Ling-Fei. 'You know that.'

Lance felt like a fool and a failure. 'We'll try again tomorrow,' said Ling-Fei, giving him a kind smile. 'And who knows? Maybe by then your power will have awakened on its own.'

Lance nodded and tried to smile, but he couldn't fake it.

It is all right, thought Infinity. *I know your power will come.*

I hope so, Lance thought back, grateful that they could communicate through their bond and didn't have to say anything out loud.

Zoe squeezed his hand. 'Don't worry, Lance,' she said. It felt strange to have his little sister comforting him, but he appreciated it all the same.

'You all did great today,' said Billy. 'You too, Lance. I know it probably doesn't feel like it, but as Ling-Fei said sometimes strengthening the bond and awakening your powers takes time. Don't let it get to you.'

Lance couldn't believe that he'd failed so spectacularly in front of the person he most wanted to impress.

'Thanks, Billy,' he managed to say, but he couldn't look him in the eye.

'Tomorrow me and Spark can work with you and Infinity,' Billy offered. 'Ling-Fei is the expert, but Spark and I know a thing or two about awakening powers right, Spark?'

'Yes,' said Spark, fixing Lance with her powerful gaze. 'And I can sense that when Lance's power does awaken, it will be one unlike we have ever seen before.'

That cheered Lance up a little bit. Spark was a seer dragon after all, and if she said he would have a good power, it had to be true.

At least he hoped so.

*

After their class with Ling-Fei, they flew to the Labs, arriving at a huge glass and steel building with halls big enough for even the larger dragons to fit inside. All along the sides were lab tables covered in tons of interesting equipment where the human members of the Dragon Force worked.

Lance was expecting to see Jordan, but he and Midnight weren't there. Another Dragon Force member welcomed them instead, one Lance had never met. She had light brown skin and a long black braid, and she was extremely enthusiastic.

'Hi!' she said, beaming at them. 'I'm Divya. I'm a newer member of the Dragon Force, and I help out in the Labs. I'll be leading your session today. Usually Jordan runs the Labs classes, but he and Midnight were called out this morning because of an attack in London.'

Lance and Zoe exchanged a worried look.

'Is everything okay?' Lance asked. 'Our parents live in London.' He hoped they were safe.

'Oh, it's nothing that Jordan and Midnight can't handle. Your parents will be totally fine. Our Dragon Force detection tech works so well that we're usually alerted to unusual activity before any humans are impacted. Jordan and Midnight are very good at their jobs. They'll get there, deal with whatever creature has decided to cause chaos and be back at Camp Claw in time for dinner.'

'Can we call our parents?' Zoe asked in a quiet voice.

'I wish you could, but we have to be really strict about our no-contact-with-the-outside-world rule at Camp Claw. We can't risk anything being compromised or shared. I'm sorry!' Divya sounded truly apologetic. 'But I promise your parents will be safe.'

'Okay,' said Zoe, and Lance slung an arm round her shoulder.

'Mum and Dad are fine,' he whispered. 'Jordan won't let anything happen to them or the rest of London.'

Zoe nodded, and Lance could tell she was trying to be brave.

Lance had hoped his power would awaken in the Labs, but it quickly became clear he was not a natural at molecule magic. Divya showed them how the Heart Stone sent pulses of magic towards the Labs, and how they were able to harness that magic and use it to power Camp Claw's technology. She also showed them the glass room where the Dragon Force stored its source of golden elixir. It was only enough to fill a cup, and it floated in the middle of the room.

'We only need a tiny drop of golden elixir to imbue power into an object,' Divya explained. 'It's extremely potent. As far as we know, this is the very last elixir in the whole world. Some members of the Dragon Force have been tasked with searching for more, which might have fallen into the New World during the Great Collapse, but we haven't found it yet.'

Then Divya led them into a 'molecular magic cube'. 'This room contains trace amounts of golden elixir, which will allow anyone, even those without a natural affinity for molecule magic, to manipulate molecules. Those with natural molecule magic will have their powers heightened.' Divya gave everyone an encouraging smile. 'I'm sure you'll all make something amazing!'

Bea took a sheet of paper and manipulated the molecules so it reverted into plant matter. With a flick of her hand, the plant matter reassembled into a small tree in the middle of the room.

Divya applauded. 'Wonderful!' she said approvingly. 'I can tell you have an aptitude for molecule magic by how well you manipulated the molecules and created something new!'

Zoe was able to freeze water molecules, creating an ice sculpture, and Arthur used the golden elixir to change his body density so he was able to float.

With some help from Divya, Lance was able to start a small fire from the oxygen and nitrogen in the air. But this felt completely useless in the company of dragons, since they were all more than capable of making fires themselves.

Lance left the Labs feeling even more frustrated. He was letting the Dragon Force down.

'Your power will awaken soon, I'm sure of it,' Zoe said as they walked out of the Labs and went down to the Palm to have lunch in the canteen. Lance gave her a half-hearted smile.

But at lunch, lots of the other recruits came over

to Lance to say how lucky he was that he'd already found his dragon, and he realized he really *was* lucky. He had Infinity. And nothing was going to change that.

He sent a burst of affection towards her down their bond.

I'm so glad I have you by my side now.

Now and for ever, Infinity thought back. *We are a team.*

Lance looked up at his friends, who were all busy eating. 'I'm sorry for being so grumpy,' he said, feeling a little embarrassed about how he'd been acting. 'I just really want to know what my power is.'

'That's okay,' said Bea, taking another bite of her ham sandwich. 'I understand. I would be grumpy too if I didn't have my power yet!'

'Oh, absolutely,' Arthur added. 'If I had to sit around while all your powers had awakened, I wouldn't just be grumpy, I'd be glaring at each of you so much you'd think super-glaring was my power and I was trying to blast you with my eyes.'

Lance laughed. 'I'm glad you guys get it.' He grinned at his friends. 'You all have such awesome powers. I guess I'm a little intimidated. I just hope my power is worth the wait.'

After lunch, the four friends met up with their dragons again and flew to the Water Jungle for their first class with Lola. She waved at them as they landed in the shimmering turquoise water. Neptune was next to Lola, with only her head poking out of the water. She was even bigger up close, and Lance found himself feeling a little nervous at being so near to such a giant dragon.

Zoe let out a delighted laugh. 'Violet, your scales look even more beautiful in this water!'

'My scales always look beautiful,' said Violet. 'But I agree, they look especially nice here.'

'How about my scales?' said Infinity mischievously, shifting her scales to match Violet's. Only her four gemstones stayed their original colour.

'An improvement, I would say,' said Violet, tossing her head.

'A nice trick,' said Neon gruffly.

Lance knew the big dragon was trying to be friendly, but he could feel through their bond that

Neon's comment had made Infinity embarrassed. She quickly shifted back to her orange scales.

'It's more than a nice trick,' said Lola. 'Camouflage can be very useful. I'm glad to see that you've mastered it so well, Infinity.'

It was slightly strange to Lance how Infinity was still learning what her true powers were, just like him, but he also found it comforting. They were going through this together. He gave Infinity a reassuring pat.

'Since you four already have your heart bonds, you're ready for your first water class,' Lola went on. 'Now, until you've passed your water exams, you're not allowed to go in the Water Jungle without a member of the Dragon Force. The waters may appear gentle, but they can change quickly, and while most creatures who have made their home in the Water Jungle are friendly, occasionally the more dangerous ones make an appearance. Is that understood?'

Everyone nodded.

'Of course there's more danger,' said Arthur. 'Is there anywhere at Camp Claw that *isn't* dangerous?'

'Your pods,' said Lola with a wry grin. 'That's probably it.'

'Noted,' said Arthur. 'And here I was thinking this was the safest place in the New World because it's the home of the Dragon Force.'

'You're probably safer here than anywhere else,' said Lola, sounding unexpectedly serious. 'Especially with the rise in attacks in the New World.'

'Do you know what's causing the increase in attacks?' asked Lance.

Lola shook her head. 'No. All we know is there's been an increase in what we call "disturbances", and there have been even more monstrous creatures for us to deal with recently.' She laughed a little. 'I hope you all master your powers soon so you can help us out! Anyway, back to the lesson – I'm assuming you all know how to swim?'

Everyone nodded again.

'First, I want us to practise diving without dragons. If you ever find yourself separated from your dragon in a water battle, you need to be able to get to the surface, and quickly. Most likely your dragon will have enchanted you to ensure you can breathe under water, but enchantments can wear off. Who wants to dive first?'

'Me!' cried Zoe. 'I love diving!'

Lola grinned at her enthusiasm. 'That's great, but make sure you're careful because there are rocks—'

But Zoe wasn't listening – she was already clambering up Violet's back and then diving headfirst into the water. A moment later, she popped back up, face contorted in pain.

'Zoe!' Lance swam over to his sister, who was holding her elbow. Blood was seeping between her fingers.

'As I was saying,' said Lola, 'there are rocks in the water that are hard to see, and they have razor-sharp edges that can cut through a super-suit. Zoe, are you all right?'

'It really stings,' Zoe admitted.

'Let me heal you,' said Violet, who had appeared by her side in an instant. 'Here, climb on my back again.'

Lance helped his sister clamber onto Violet, and then the purple dragon slowly lifted into the air and began to flap her gauzy wings. Seconds later, lavender-coloured mist flowed out of her scales, and

Lance watched in awe as Zoe's cut, and her super-suit, stitched back together, as if by magic, which he supposed it was.

Lola was watching Violet closely. 'I didn't realize you were a healer dragon,' she said, surprised. 'We always need more healer dragons.'

Violet let out a sharp laugh. 'You are probably surprised because I do not have the friendly, caring demeanour of Buttons.' She flashed her teeth. 'And I do not heal like him either. My mist heals, but it also hypnotizes and harms.'

Lola looked impressed. 'Remind me never to get on your bad side.' Then she turned to Zoe. 'I'm sorry you hurt yourself, but you brilliantly demonstrated one of the first rules of water battle – always check your surroundings. You never know what might be hiding right beneath the surface.'

Suddenly there was a loud blaring sound. It was the most deafening alarm Lance had heard at Camp Claw. And from the expression on Lola's face, he knew it wasn't good.

A small floating fireball appeared above Lola's head, and Lance realized it was flame post. *The*

Dragon Force must use it for internal messaging too, he thought to himself. The flame post unravelled, but this wasn't like the one that had arrived in Lance's bedroom and formed words in the air. Instead, this unfurled like a letter and only Lola could see what was written on it. Whatever she read, she didn't like, because her mouth took on the shape of a flat line, and she stiffened.

'I'm sorry, recruits, but I have to cut the class short. Neptune and I need to leave immediately to deal with an emergency in the New World.'

'It isn't in London, is it?' Lance burst out. 'I know Jordan's there now because of a disturbance!'

Lola shook her head. 'No, it isn't in London. This one's in Japan. Something has come out of the sea. Our tech can't tell what it is, but it's enormous and it's causing tsunamis. Neptune and I need to deal with it. We'll go via water portal, so you all need to get out of the Water Jungle and head back to the Volcano. You're not allowed to be here without Dragon Force supervision.'

'You two stay safe,' said Neon. 'We will look out for our humans while you are gone.'

'We will do our best,' said Neptune. Lola held onto her spikes and the pair dived down into the depths of the Water Jungle.

'Come,' said Neon to the recruits. 'We will take you all back to the Volcano. You should stay there for the rest of the day. You will be safest there.'

As Neon and Bea led the way back to the Volcano, Lance followed on Infinity's back, trying to ignore his rising trepidation.

What was happening in the outside world that meant several of the elite Dragon Force team had been called away in quick succession to deal with different emergencies?

Back at the Volcano, the group split up. Zoe said she needed a nap after the adrenaline rush caused by her accident and Bea wanted to practise her molecule magic to see if she could make light bulbs change colour. Meanwhile, Arthur, with a slightly strange expression on his face, said he was heading to his room to work on his map magic.

Neon and Jaws decided to go to the Tower to get more information about the increase in attacks in the New World, and Violet told everyone she would be sunning herself on the beach.

That left Lance and Infinity standing at the base of the Volcano. Instead of going to his pod or the common room, Lance wanted to work on strengthening his heart bond with his dragon, hopefully awakening his power in the process. Infinity seemed to have the same thought.

'I do not know why we all had to come back here,' she said. 'You are perfectly safe anywhere in Dragon's Claw as long as you are with your dragon!'

'That's what I was thinking!' Lance gave Infinity a mischievous grin. 'Maybe you and I could head to one of the claws and try to awaken my power?'

Infinity tilted her head to the side, considering her human's request. 'That would be directly breaking an order from a Dragon Force member,' she said, sounding a little anxious. 'But I do want to show you more of the claws ... We will be careful, yes?'

'Of course!' said Lance.

'I know,' said Infinity, clearly warming to the idea. 'We will not land anywhere. We will just stay in the air. That way we can say we didn't go anywhere else, not really.'

'Excellent plan,' said Lance.

'And . . .' Infinity suddenly shifted her scales to sky-blue. 'I suppose it would not hurt for me to blend in with the sky. Just in case anyone looked up.'

Lance laughed. 'Infinity, you're a genius!'

'I am a dragon,' said Infinity with a wide grin. 'Of course I am a genius.'

Lance leaped on his dragon's back, and the two of them took to the sky.

Infinity swooped and soared high above Dragon's Claw. She was careful to avoid certain air spaces, and Lance remembered what she'd said about knowing Dragon's Claw better than anyone else. She certainly knew how to blend in and get around undetected. It made him wonder if she was hiding any other secrets from the Dragon Force. Or him . . .

'Oh, look at the Mirage!' said Infinity. 'There is a storm inside it! I will take you closer for a better look.'

The Mirage was the claw Lance was the most

anxious about, but he trusted Infinity. If she said they could get closer, then she knew what she was doing.

The Mirage looked like a canyon filled with clouds, and right now mini whirlpools of lightning filled each one. The colour had changed too – now the Mirage was a pale mint green with streaks of silver and gold throughout it. In the very centre, it looked like six lines stretched from one side to the other, like guitar strings.

'What do you see?' asked Infinity curiously.

'What do you mean?' asked Lance. 'Don't you see the same thing?'

'The Mirage looks a little different to everyone,' Infinity explained. 'That is part of the reason it is so dangerous.'

Lance told her what he could see and Infinity laughed. 'That is wonderful.' He was about to ask her what she saw when Infinity went very still. 'There is a human down there, by the edge. They should not be there.'

Lance peered closer and gasped. 'Wait a minute – I think that's Arthur! What is he doing there?'

'I do not know, but it is dangerous. Come on!'

Infinity zoomed down from the sky, so fast that Lance was worried she would knock straight into Arthur and he would fall into the Mirage.

'Arthur! What are you doing?' Lance shouted. Arthur was so surprised he stumbled. Lance reached out and grabbed his friend's hand, pulling Arthur up behind him so they were now both riding Infinity, who had soared back into the sky.

'You know the Mirage is off-limits!' said Lance.

'Well, what are *you* doing here?' replied Arthur.

'Saving you!' Infinity exclaimed. 'Jaws is going to be furious when he finds out his human came to the Mirage without him! You could have fallen in and been lost for ever!'

'I can't get lost, remember?' said Arthur, sounding smug. 'I have my pathfinder magic. I was mapping Dragon's Claw in my mind, then I saw this short cut that led to the Mirage and I wanted to try it.'

'Arthur, even most of us dragons cannot go into the Mirage,' said Infinity, sounding uncharacteristically stern. 'Just because you have pathfinder magic, it does not mean you would not have been lost in there.'

'I only wanted to explore,' said Arthur petulantly.

Suddenly, there was a sharp beep, so piercing it hurt Lance's ears. A moment later, he heard the strange humming, which he now associated with danger.

'What was that noise?' said Infinity. 'That beep? I do not like it!' Lance knew that Infinity could hear the humming too.

'Nothing,' said Arthur, and Lance saw him tuck his nutrition remote into a pocket in his super-suit.

'You are lying, Arthur,' said Infinity bluntly. 'I can sense that thing you just hid away is bad. We need to take it to Billy to look at.'

'No!' said Arthur, and to Lance's shock, he threw the remote into the Mirage far below them.

'That was weird,' said Lance, confused by Arthur's erratic behaviour.

'I just . . . it's personal, okay? It has information on it about me. I didn't want Billy or any of the Dragon Force looking at it.'

'I still think we need to tell them,' said Infinity, sounding anxious. 'Even if it means Lance and I will get in trouble for flying over Dragon's Claw when we should have stayed at the Volcano. What was that thing, Arthur? It felt . . . wrong.'

'It doesn't matter. I don't need it any more,' Arthur said in a small voice. 'Please don't tell Billy and the rest of the Dragon Force. I know I wasn't supposed to be bring anything with me from home, but it's gone now.'

'That's for sure,' said Lance, glancing over into the abyss of the Mirage again. He couldn't work out why Arthur had destroyed his nutrition remote. Something wasn't adding up.

'Can we go back to the Volcano?' said Arthur. 'I promise I won't try to path-find on my own again. Lesson learned.'

Lance could tell Infinity was torn.

'Please?' Arthur asked again.

'It is up to Lance,' said Infinity.

'Me?' Lance didn't want this responsibility. He didn't want to get Arthur in trouble while admitting he and Infinity had broken the rules, but he also didn't want to ignore his dragon's gut feeling.

But then they saw a familiar shape in the sky, and the decision was made for them. It was Spark, with

Billy on his back. Right next to them were Xing and Ling-Fei.

Spark and Xing swooped down low enough for Lance to see Billy was frowning.

'What are you three doing way out here?' said Billy, eyeing them suspiciously. 'You're supposed to be back at the Volcano.'

'I was practising my pathfinding magic,' Arthur said quickly. 'Sorry, I know I should have stayed in my pod or the common room. Infinity and Lance found me and were about to bring me back. It's my fault.'

Billy frowned. 'And what were you two doing?'

Lance got a funny feeling in his stomach. Arthur wasn't lying, but he wasn't telling the whole truth either. He knew dragons could read human's hearts, but could they tell when humans were being dishonest too?

'I wanted to see if flying would awaken my power,' said Lance. It was another half-truth.

Billy sighed and brushed his hair out of his eyes. 'Lance, I know how desperate you are to awaken your power, but there's a lot going on right now. I need you guys to stay safe. You're not in trouble, but you do need to go back to the Volcano right now.'

'Where are you four going?' Lance couldn't help but ask. 'You look like you're in a hurry.'

'There's been another attack in the New World. A big one. It needs both of us and our dragons to handle it.' Billy shook his head. 'Something strange is going on. There have always been disturbances since the Great Collapse, but things have escalated in the past week in a way that doesn't make sense.'

'But Lola just left too,' spluttered Lance. 'You can't all leave Dragon's Claw!'

'Don't worry, Lance,' said Ling-Fei. 'Dylan and Buttons are still here, and so are Divya and the other Dragon Force members. You're all safe here. We'll be back before you know it, and then we can work together on awakening your power. How does that sound?'

Lance began to hear humming, the one Infinity called a warning song, even louder than it had been moments before. He could tell the stars didn't want Billy and Ling-Fei to leave. But how could he explain that? For a moment, he almost said something, but then Billy glanced up at the portal Spark had just opened behind them, and decided to keep it to himself. The world needed the Dragon Force more than Lance did.

So instead, he nodded. 'Okay,' he said. 'See you later.'

'Don't get into any trouble while we're gone!' cried Billy.

A few seconds later, Billy and Ling-Fei zoomed through the portal on the backs of their dragons, and the portal closed behind them as if it'd never been there at all.

'So are you going to tell anyone else what happened?' Arthur asked as they flew back to the Volcano.

Lance didn't like keeping secrets from his sister, but the remote was Arthur's secret to share, not Lance's. He wouldn't keep everything from Zoe though.

'We should tell Zoe and Bea we saw Billy and Ling-Fei leaving,' Lance said firmly. 'And you should tell Jaws you snuck out to practise pathfinding magic. We already told Billy anyway.'

Arthur sighed. 'I suppose you're right.'

'Something still feels wrong to me,' Infinity cut in.

'You heard Billy,' said Lance. 'There's been an increase in attacks in the New World. Of course something feels wrong.'

'That must be it,' said Infinity, but Billy could tell she was unsettled, and that made him feel unsettled too.

The rest of the day felt strange. Everyone was on edge, knowing that Billy and the elite Dragon Force members had left Dragon's Claw. It was as if they were all waiting for something to happen, but they weren't sure what.

After a quiet dinner, where Lance and Arthur recounted the earlier events for Zoe and Bea, they all went to bed early. Things would be better in the morning, Lance told himself. But as he drifted off to sleep, the stars' warning song echoed in his ears.

The Attack

Lance woke up to the sound of an alarm and the sight of flashing lights. What time was it? As he sat up, rubbing the sleep from his eyes, he was horrified to see the flashing lights weren't coming from the alarm but from explosions outside his pod. He sprang out of bed and saw that Dragon's Claw was under attack. There must have been over a hundred creatures outside battling the Dragon Force riders.

Lance darted over to his balcony door, but ran straight into the force field with a *thud*.

'Ow,' he said, rubbing his arm. 'Pod, let me out.'

'An external disturbance has been reported. All

exits have been locked. Please remain in your room and stay calm,' the pod responded robotically.

'What?' replied Lance in disbelief. 'I said, let me out!'

'I am sorry, Lance Lo. Your pod currently poses the least amount of risk to your health and safety. The exits will remain locked.'

Lance hurried over to his front door. His hand couldn't pass through the force field here either.

'Lance, are you in there?'

Lance immediately recognized his sister's voice. 'Zoe! What are you doing out there?'

'Bea used her powers to deactivate my room's force field. Look . . .' She paused. 'I know you're not going to like this, but Bea and I need to help defend Dragon's Claw.'

'*What?* Zoe, you have to stay in the Volcano. It's too dangerous out there.'

'This is the whole reason we're at Camp Claw!' she replied. 'We're training to join the Dragon Force and the team needs our help now. Most of the elite members are out fighting other battles and Dragon's Claw needs to be defended. It's our duty!'

'You're too young to have duties! You're staying in

here with me,' Lance said, his voice tight. He was frustrated, but more than that, scared for his sister. Surely she wasn't going to go off into battle?

'I'm sorry, Lance,' his sister said firmly.

'Let me out. If you insist on leaving the Volcano, I'm coming with you.'

There was another pause. 'Lance, you don't have your power yet. You won't be able to defend yourself properly.'

'I have Infinity,' he said with an indignant huff.

'Her ability to change colour isn't going to keep you safe.'

Lance was flabbergasted. Was his little sister really about to run headfirst into danger and leave him behind for his own safety? 'Zoe, you are *not* going out there without me! And you know Infinity is much more than just a colour-changing dragon!'

'I'm sorry, Lance. Bea and I can actually help in this situation. Our dragons, bonds and powers are strong. I'll come back when it's safe.' She paused again. 'I'm sure we won't be very long.'

'Zoe! Don't you dare go! Let me out!' Lance shouted through the door.

The only reply he received was the siren still going off in his room.

Lance felt his throat tighten and tears prickle his eyes. 'ZOE, COME BACK! YOU CAN'T GO OUT THERE ALONE!' He slammed his fists on the force field, over and over again. But it was no use. It didn't budge. In desperation, Lance grabbed the handle of his erhu and slammed the hammer-shaped end of the instrument against the force field.

BOOM.

Instead of breaking in half, the erhu smashed straight through the force field. Lance gazed in amazement as the force field flickered and faded away. He looked at the erhu still in one piece in his hands. It was shimmering, and Lance swore he could feel it thrumming, as if trying to communicate with him. He brought the erhu closer to his face, trying to make sense of what had just happened. He could feel energy inside the erhu. An energy that felt familiar somehow. He nearly dropped the instrument when he recognized what it was. It was *him*. It was the same wild and free energy he felt when he lost himself in a song. He had somehow transferred his own energy into the erhu when he'd picked it up and slammed it into the force field. He gripped the instrument tighter, with purpose this time, and opened his heart, letting his energy flow into the erhu. The instrument started to glow in his hands.

Lance smiled. He'd discovered his power. It was so obvious now, he felt silly for not realizing it sooner. It made complete sense that his power would have something to do with music. He strummed a long, sombre note on the erhu, and smoke-like wisps of gold and orange flowed from the strings into the air. The instrument glowed even brighter. He wasn't sure what the limits or rules of his power were, but for now he knew he had a magic erhu and there wasn't any time to waste.

He turned towards his balcony door and flung the erhu at it. The instrument smashed straight through the force field and swung back into the room into Lance's hand like a boomerang. His smile broadened. He wouldn't be left behind – and now he could help.

Lance ran with his erhu onto his balcony and leaped off. He called down their bond, *Infinity, I'm out! Let's ride!* In an instant, Infinity was under him, and the two of them flew into battle.

Through their bond, Lance quickly shared what had happened with his erhu.

'I knew it was meant for you,' Infinity said when he had finished. 'I cannot wait to see how you use it!'

'I think that's going to happen sooner rather than later!' Lance said as a giant ball of flaming rock came straight at them.

Lance flung his erhu at it, and the flying rock exploded into dust. He stretched his hand out, and the erhu boomeranged back to him.

Infinity roared with glee.

'Lance Lo, did you just explode that fire ball?' cried a voice from above. It was Dylan O'Donnell, riding on the back of Buttons.

'I did!' Lance called back.

'I was going to order you back to your pod, but now I've seen what you can do, I think you should stay and help.'

'You got it!' said Lance. 'And watch out!' Another giant ball of flaming rock was heading straight towards Dylan and Buttons. Lance flung his erhu out again and the rock exploded into smithereens.

'That's seriously impressive,' said Dylan.

'Where are the others?' Lance asked, looking around for Zoe and Bea.

'The rest of the recruits are safely in their pods, except your sister and Bea, who are in the Palm with Kronos. And Divya and her dragon are trying to fix our defence system. But that's it. We're a skeleton crew. The rest of the Dragon Force squad went to different areas in the New World to help with the huge number of global attacks. We thought Camp Claw would be fine. We've never been attacked here before. I don't know how those things are getting through our force field defences.'

'What things?' asked Lance anxiously.

'*Those* things,' said Buttons gravely, pointing his claw towards the beach.

Lance looked and gasped. Rising out of the sea was an enormous lava creature, almost as tall as the Volcano itself. It was made entirely of lava rocks with glowing molten lava flowing between the cracks. Its broad shoulders were covered with huge, jagged spikes that went all the way down its back, and its hands were so hot they were covered in flames, molten lava dripping from its fingertips.

'What is that?' Lance croaked, trying to mask the trepidation he felt.

'A very grumpy lava monster,' said Dylan grimly. 'It can shoot out lava and pieces of itself like exploding magma cannonballs. And if that wasn't enough, it can also regenerate. Are you sure you want to stick around?'

Lance clenched his jaw. 'This is why I'm here.' It was true. This was his moment to prove himself. To show the Dragon Force he was meant to be at Camp Claw and deserved a spot on their elite team.

Infinity roared in response. 'I have hidden for too long. I am ready now to fight for—'

'Watch out!' cried Dylan, pointing behind them.

Lance felt a blast of heat as Infinity swung to one side. To his horror, a stream of molten lava clipped one of Infinity's wings, and she roared in pain.

'Above us!' cried Lance.

A huge fist made of rock came flying down towards them, but this time Lance and Infinity were prepared. He leaned into Infinity and the two of them swooped out of the way, touching down on the beach.

Lance leaped off his dragon. 'Infinity, you're hurt!' He felt panicked and scared and desperate to help her.

'I do not know if I can fly,' Infinity admitted, and Lance felt her pain down their bond. 'That second lava monster came out of nowhere.'

The lava monsters didn't seem to be able to fly, but they were so gigantic that the best way to battle them was in flight.

'You'll be okay,' he said. She had to be.

Lance looked up and saw it was indeed a second lava monster that had sneaked up behind them. The two beasts were closing in.

'Over here, you rotten rock trolls!'

Lance looked to the new voice and saw his sister flying towards them on Violet. Zoe started replicating herself, and dozens of Zoe copies leaped off Violet's back. Some ran directly at the lava monsters, while others jumped and flipped in all directions.

For a moment, the lava monsters were stunned, unsure who to chase. But they quickly redirected their attacks at the Zoe replicas, firing lava out of their fingertips.

Poof, poof, poof.

The Zoes vanished as they were struck by the lava.

Lance pumped his fist. 'It's working, Zoe! The lava creatures think your replicas are real. Keep distracting them!'

Buttons and Dylan landed next to Lance and Infinity in the sand.

'That was a hard hit,' said Dylan, wincing. 'I can't believe you didn't fall out of the sky.'

'I would never fall with Lance on my back,' said Infinity indignantly, and Lance felt a rush of affection for his dragon. He knew he could always count on her.

'I'll heal you,' Buttons said to Infinity.

'Make it quick,' said Dylan, looking over his shoulder. 'Those two lava monsters are closing back in on us.'

Buttons took Infinity's wing in his short paws and closed his eyes. He made a low growl that almost sounded like a purr, just like when he'd healed Violet. Lance saw the charred section of Infinity's wing repair itself as if by magic, and he could feel Infinity's relief through their bond.

Infinity gave a tentative flap of her wing. 'Like new,' she said, nodding towards Buttons in thanks.

Lance looked back to his sister, who was still replicating as fast as her power would let her. 'Where's Bea?' he shouted.

Zoe pointed. 'She's still in the Palm battling two other lava monsters with Neon and Kronos.'

One of the lava monsters let out a frustrated roar, stretching its arms out wide. A bright white light shot out between the cracks of its body, and it started to expand as if filling with lava. The rocks that it was made of began to tremble and shake, and it looked as though it would explode at any moment.

'I think it's going to self-destruct!' yelled Lance. 'Shield yourselves!'

The Swarm

Just as the monster appeared to be seconds away from bursting, it turned towards them and unleashed a flood of burning lava from its eyes and mouth. Lance and Dylan flew skywards on their dragons, narrowly missing the attack.

'That is an exceptionally unfriendly lava monster,' said Dylan, now hovering next to Zoe and Violet. 'Hopefully the others have better manners.'

Lance looked to the Palm and saw another huge lava explosion. 'We have to help Bea, Neon and Kronos. We'll be stronger together.'

'You're right,' said Dylan.

'I'll try to get these two lava monsters to chase

my replicas to the Palm so they move away from the Volcano where the other recruits are.'

'Good idea, Zoe!' said Lance, feeling proud of his sister for coming up with a way to protect the rest of the recruits.

Then they heard screams coming from the direction of the Palm.

'Sounds like they're having a hard time already!' said Lance. 'Come on, we have to go help them, quick!' He and Infinity flew towards the sound.

But it wasn't Bea but Arthur who was running from another lava monster.

'Help me!' cried Arthur.

Lance threw his erhu at the monster's head and Infinity shot out a burst of fire, but the lava creature swatted the instrument out of the air as if it were a toothpick and Infinity's flames hit its chest with little effect. Clearly the monster was much stronger than the flaming rocks it shot from its fingertips. Lance held out his hand and summoned the erhu back to him.

'Do these monsters have a weakness?' Lance shouted.

Before anyone could respond, the creature's huge

burning hand swiped down and picked up Arthur in one of its claws. He cried out in pain. Lance felt helpless. He wanted to save his friend, but he didn't know what to do.

A thunderous roar sounded behind them as a black and silver blur flashed by. Jaws opened his powerful mouth and closed his jaws around the lava monster's wrist. The beast let out a roar as its hand fell off from the powerful bite, and Jaws dived down and grabbed Arthur from the falling hand, holding him gently in his teeth until he could lay him down on the sand.

Jaws turned back towards the monster and let out another ear-splitting roar, so loud Lance swore he could see a sonic boom knocking the beast right in the chest. It fell backwards and Jaws leaped into the air, clenching his razor-sharp teeth around its neck. With a loud *crunch*, the creature's head separated from its body. Lava oozed from its neck and the monster crumbled, thousands of lifeless lava rocks falling to the sand like a rock shower.

'Arthur!' cried Jaws. 'Are you hurt?' The dragon raced over to his heart-bonded human.

Lance could see blood trickling from the sleeves of Arthur's super-suit. He knew that the suits could withstand heat and the fiercest of bites, so he didn't even want to imagine how hard the lava monster must have been holding onto his friend.

Arthur winced. 'What happened? I feel dizzy.'

Buttons flew down from above and placed both his paws on Arthur's chest. 'You're lucky Jaws was here to save you. I'll heal you now.'

As Buttons healed Arthur, Dylan gave Jaws a sharp look. 'You know, Jaws, it would have been useful if you'd done that as soon as the lava monsters showed up.'

Jaws growled in response. 'The strength of my bond with Arthur powered me up. I could not have done that without our bond. When I sensed he was hurt, something woke inside me, and I felt more powerful than ever before. I do not know if can do it again.'

Dylan nodded. 'Fair enough. They're enormously powerful creatures. Annoyingly so. I tried using my charm to make them leave, but I might as well have been talking to a rock.' He let out a humourless laugh. 'Which I suppose I was.' He sighed as he adjusted his glasses.

'Look out behind you!' said Bea.

Lance turned and saw his sister's replicas had managed to trick the three remaining lava monsters into chasing them around the Palm, but they seemed to be quickly figuring out how her power worked, because they were abandoning the replicas and heading towards the real humans and dragons. Bea had changed course and was chasing the monsters on Neon's back and Kronos was right behind them. Lance was relieved that Arthur had been healed, but the bigger problem of how they were going to defeat all the creatures remained.

Zoe turned to her dragon. 'They aren't interested in my replicas any more. Maybe we can hypnotize them with your powers.' She closed her eyes and placed her hands on Violet, clearly speaking with her dragon through their bond. 'I'll try to supercharge you,' she said aloud.

Violet nodded and her eyes grew big and round as they began to glow a deep purple. Her body started to twist and swirl like an optical illusion, and Lance felt drawn in. Then Violet's scales started shedding and floating in the air like shimmering flower petals.

The group of three lava monsters stopped in their tracks, transfixed by Violet. They swayed slightly in place. The fire in their eyes and the glow coming from their bodies seemed to dim like a flame being extinguished until their glow disappeared completely.

'Finish them, Bea!' Zoe cried as loudly as she could.

Bea nodded and put her hands on Neon's back, and the dragon's eyes flashed an electric green. Neon spun in a tight circle and slammed his tail down on the ground in the direction of the three entranced creatures. An electric shockwave moved through the earth, rippling the surface of the ground as it went, soon hitting the beasts. Electricity flowed up from their feet to their heads, and they exploded in a cloud of dust and ash.

'We did it! We defeated the lava monsters!' Lance said as he, his friends and their dragons settled together in the Palm.

'Yes,' said Bea. 'But I don't think Neon's blast would have worked if Zoe and Violet hadn't weakened them first.' She flew over to them. 'The way you hypnotized those monsters was amazing!'

Violet gave Zoe a toothy grin. 'You really ruffled my scales there, child. I have never been able to shed them in that way before.'

'Consider yourself supercharged,' said Zoe, patting her dragon on the back.

Dylan breathed a sigh of relief. 'Well done, everyone. I'm so glad you're all okay. Typical that the one time we have a security breach is when I'm left in charge. I don't even understand how those creatures got into Dragon's Claw. Nothing is meant to be able to get past our defences.'

'I can tell you how,' came an unexpected voice from above.

Lance looked up and gasped. A strange creature had appeared in the sky. It looked like a huge centaur, but instead of its body being half-human and half-horse, the creature was half-human and half-beetle. From the waist up, it was completely human, but from the waist down, the creature had a beetle's body with two large claws at the front and hard shell wings that buzzed as it flew. The beetle-man was completely gold, and surrounding him were hundreds of normal-sized gold beetles. His expression of glee made him even more terrifying to look at.

'I've waited a long time to come to Camp Claw. I never received an invite and it was impossible to access without one with all your tech. But my lava monsters and I managed to break in with the help of a *friend*.'

Infinity shifted underneath him. *Lance! Do you hear the humming?*

Lance's blood went cold. Even with the beetle-man speaking, he could hear the strange sound. *Yes*, he replied. This was no ordinary monstrous creature. This was something else, something worse, and the stars were trying to warn Lance.

'Frank Albert?' Dylan burst out incredulously. 'Is that you?'

'Oh, so you do recognize me!' said the creature. 'Or at least, who I used to be. Frank Albert was lost long ago when you and your Dragon Force buddies left me for dead in the In-Between.' The beetle-man frowned. 'How absolutely dreadful it is to see you again, Dylan O'Donnell. I bet you thought I'd never make it out.' He gave a hideous laugh. 'But here I am! The In-Between swallowed me up and drowned me in a river of golden elixir, but I was reborn as the glorious creature you see before you. I am no longer Frank Albert. I am now the Swarm. When the Human and Dragon realms became one after the Great Collapse, no one was more delighted about it than me. I quickly seized the opportunity to escape the In-Between, and I've been waiting patiently ever since for my chance to take revenge on you awful kids and the dragons who did this to me. Now nothing can stop me!' The Swarm cackled again.

'Frank Albert?' said Arthur, blinking in disbelief. 'You're Frank Albert? The man behind TURBO technology?'

'Oh, hello, little widdle Arthur,' the Swarm said in a mocking baby voice. 'Surprised to see me? I suppose I should be thanking you!'

'No ... Surely not ...' Arthur began to shake all over.

'It gives me great pleasure to say it's one of your own who's been deceiving you,' the Swarm announced to the group, grinning wickedly. 'You should've let that sorry excuse of a human suffer in the hand of my lava monster.'

Jaws lowered his head and let out a low snarl.

The Swarm pouted. 'How sweet of Arthur's dragon to be so protective of him,' he said with a laugh. 'But would you act the same if you knew your human was the reason I was able to break through Dragon's Claw's defences?'

'What?' said Lance, outraged by the Swarm's statement. 'There's no way that's true!'

But when he turned to Arthur, he saw that he'd turned as white as a sheet and was trembling uncontrollably.

'I . . . I didn't mean to,' Arthur stammered. 'He told me he was a friend of my dad's, and all I needed to do was bring the remote with me. I never thought he was going to attack. And I didn't think he was . . . whatever this is!'

The Swarm spat. 'You were so easy to fool. I was never a friend of your father. Quite the opposite. When I fell out of the In-Between, I was in a chrysalis form. I floated in the sea, trapped in a hard shell, with only my own thoughts to keep me company. But as soon as I emerged as this, the Swarm, I realized I needed tech to take down the Dragon Force. TURBO, my own company, had been dismantled, and much of the tech had been sold to Royden Enterprises, so I paid Peter Royden a little visit. I asked him to see sense – that with his tech and my powers, we could destroy the Dragon Force and dragonkind once and for all. But he refused me!' The Swarm grimaced. 'Nobody says no to the Swarm!'

Lance looked over at Arthur and saw his friend staring at the Swarm with an expression of pure terror. The Swarm pointed one of his pincers at Arthur.

'Everyone said your father was killed by a dragon, but did you ever see the body? Dragon claw marks look remarkably like the marks of my own claws!' The Swarm laughed again. 'I killed your father, Arthur. How do you think I got his watch? I killed him, and I took his watch. And then I broke into Royden Enterprises, and I stole all the tech I needed. I even improved it. But I still needed a way in to

Dragon's Claw, and that's where you came in, you little brat. You were so sad and so desperate. And when I gave you the remote, which could dismantle force fields but only from within, you took it. You made sure my lava monsters and I were able to break in. And even before we arrived, once the force fields were dismantled, we were able to tinker with your tech from afar!' He cackled. 'I took great delight in tampering with Camp Claw.'

Lance suddenly remembered how Dylan's control pad had frozen when he'd been testing Zoe's heart bond in the Arena. It must have been the Swarm!

Arthur made a retching sound as if he might be sick.

'Nice speech, Frank Swarm, or whatever you go by now,' said Dylan. 'But if you think we're going to allow a giant gold beetle-man to roam freely around the New World, you're wrong. Neon, trap him!'

But as Neon shot out an electric net, the Swarm cackled, showing too many teeth. 'I can't be contained so easily. In fact, I can't be contained by anything!' He sent out a blast of power from one of his claws and it blocked Neon's electric net in mid-air.

'You're all fools,' said the Swarm. 'You were far too easily distracted by my darling lava friends. You didn't even notice me taking this – the real reason I broke into Dragon's Claw.' From under his beetle body, the Swarm took out something Lance recognized right away, making his stomach plummet. It was the Heart Stone.

'NO!' shouted Infinity, zooming towards the Swarm with Lance on her back. But the Swarm sent his gold beetles towards them, so many that Infinity couldn't get past.

Through the storm of beetles, Lance saw the still-cackling Swarm use the Heart Stone to open a portal in the sky. Within seconds, he'd disappeared inside the portal, taking the stone with him.

A Dangerous Secret

Arthur let out a strangled cry, like a wounded animal, and then burst into tears.

'I'm so sorry! This is all my fault! I didn't mean for any of this to happen, I swear it! You have to believe me!'

'I don't understand,' said Dylan sharply. 'I need you to explain yourself, Arthur.' Lance could tell Dylan was trying to control his temper. He was usually so jovial, even in the face of danger, and it was strange to see him angry.

Arthur wiped his nose on his sleeve. 'When my dad died . . .' His voice cracked and he took a deep breath.

'It's all right,' said Bea comfortingly. 'Just breathe.'

'It's not all right,' muttered Dylan. 'Frank Albert, aka the Swarm, has the Heart Stone, which is what powers the whole of Dragon's Claw. Our entire defence system has been weakened.'

'Arthur just found out his father was murdered by that beetle-man creature,' Jaws growled. 'You could be a little kinder.'

Dylan let out a frustrated sigh. 'I'm trying, Jaws. I really am. I'm truly sorry about your dad, Arthur. It must be a huge shock.'

Lance couldn't imagine hearing news like that. He was glad Arthur had Jaws next to him and hoped his dragon was a comfort.

Arthur looked up with red-rimmed eyes. 'After my dad was killed, I hated dragons more than anything. I was terrified of them. I thought they were evil, all of them. It was only when . . .' His voice broke again. 'It was only when I bonded with Jaws that I began to realize I had been wrong about dragons, but by then it was too late.'

'Too late for what?' asked Zoe.

'Tell us, Arthur. Tell us everything you can,' said Neon.

Arthur took a deep, shuddering breath. 'The night I received my flame post, another letter appeared. A real letter. It arrived on my windowsill with a box. In the box was a remote powered by Royden technology, along with my dad's watch. I would have recognized it anywhere because it had my birthdate engraved on the back. The letter was signed by Frank Albert. It said he'd been there with my dad when he'd died, that my dad and him had been working together when the dragon attacked. The letter explained my dad's last words were to ask Frank to give me the watch and tell me to seek revenge on dragonkind for what they did to him. Frank said he hated dragons too, and that he'd help me in my mission for revenge. He told me to accept the invitation to Camp Claw, bring the remote with me, poke around as much as I could, and he'd take it from there.'

Lance gasped. 'Your nutrition remote is a *spy gadget*?' He couldn't believe it. How could Arthur have done this? 'Is that why you were in *my* room that first day?'

Arthur nodded, looking miserable. 'Frank

instructed me to investigate as many areas of Camp Claw as I could. He said that the remote would give me access, but I didn't know it was impacting the force fields!'

He sniffed loudly and wiped his nose on his sleeve.

'Even though I didn't know exactly what the remote was, I started to suspect it was bad. Really bad. And after I bonded with Jaws, I knew I needed to get rid of it. I didn't want revenge any more. That's why I went to the Mirage yesterday. I wanted to destroy the remote and that seemed like the best place to do it.' Arthur took another big breath. 'But I swear I had no idea Frank had become that beetle creature or that he was planning on attacking Camp Claw!'

'But what did you think he was going to do?' demanded Dylan. 'Send us presents? He said he wanted you to take revenge!'

'I don't know. I wasn't thinking properly! As soon as he mentioned my dad, I guess I lost all sense of reason. He was right – I was desperate. But now I've ended up helping the person who murdered my dad.' Arthur looked around at everyone. 'Being here made me feel better for the first time since he died, and now I've ruined everything.'

'I can't argue with that,' said Dylan, rubbing his temples. 'I wish you'd told us about the remote as soon as you started to have doubts. The Labs could have taken a look at it, worked out where it was transmitting to and potentially stopped the Swarm before it was too late.'

'He's telling us everything now,' said Buttons, coming up and patting Arthur on the back. 'That's a brave thing to do, Dylan. You were young once too.'

'I never collaborated with the enemy,' grumbled Dylan.

'But you have made mistakes. And more than that, you have forgiven others who have too. Dragons live a long time. We either have to hold grudges for ever, or we learn to forgive.'

'What happens now?' asked Lance.

'You all need to go back to your pods and stay there. I'll get in touch with Billy and the others and hope they can return in time for us to track down the Swarm and get the Heart Stone back. Without it, Dragon's Claw will be weaker than ever, so I'm going to lock it down. Nobody will be able to get in and out until the Dragon Force is back.'

As Dylan spoke, the claws themselves began to curl in on themselves, as if the land were turning into a fist.

Arthur looked at Jaws. 'I'm so sorry, Jaws. I'm the worst human you could have heart-bonded with. I understand if you want to eat me.'

'Arthur,' said Jaws, his deep voice booming. 'You have made a grave mistake, a terrible one that will have larger consequences than you ever imagined, but everyone makes mistakes. I can read your heart, and I know you are good, so you are forgiven.'

'You cannot decide that for the group!' Violet jumped in.

'No, but he is my human, and he needs to know that *I* forgive him,' Jaws insisted.

'We can fix this, Arthur,' said Lance, squatting down next to his friend. 'We'll find a way.'

Lance was hurt Arthur had lied to him, lied to all of them, but he knew Arthur hadn't meant to cause such havoc. Just the thought of how guilty and awful Arthur must be feeling made Lance feel sick to his stomach, and he wanted him to know that he wasn't alone. He had Jaws, and he had Lance and Zoe and Bea too. They could fix this together.

'You're not fixing anything,' said Dylan, glaring at them all. 'You're staying in your pods. Off you go.'

The four kids nodded, but as they made their way back to the Volcano, Lance turned and whispered to his friends, 'Meet me in the common room at midnight. I have an idea.'

The Escape

At midnight, Lance stepped out of his pyjamas into his super-suit and headed to the common room. Zoe, Bea and Arthur were already waiting for him.

'Follow me,' said Lance, and he led them through the waterfall into Infinity's secret cavern.

'Wow!' said Zoe. 'How did you find this place?'

'This is where I first met Infinity,' said Lance. 'I heard music, and I followed it here. Speaking of music, I have something to tell you guys.' Lance told them about the humming he'd been hearing since he'd arrived at Dragon's Claw. 'I think Infinity is right – the stars are trying to send us a warning. I feel it's all connected in some way – the warning song, the Swarm's attack and the increased disturbances in the New World.'

They were in the heart of the cavern now and Infinity came into sight. Lance had spoken to her through their bond and told her his plan, and she'd thought it was a good one. Now all they had to do was convince the others.

'There is another bigger cavern through here,' said Infinity, leading them down a long tunnel. 'If you call to your dragons, they will be able to fly in through this wall.'

'What? How?' said Bea.

Infinity grinned. 'Molecule magic. I can rearrange the wall's molecules so that it turns from stone to air. Dragon's Claw listens and responds to me. Sometimes I wonder if it is because we are made out of the same magic, as we were both born out of the Great Collapse.' She nodded at the children. 'Summon your dragons through your bonds.'

Moments later, Violet, Neon and Jaws burst into the Volcano.

'How is this possible?' rumbled Neon. 'I did not know about this.'

'Dragon's Claw has many secrets,' said Infinity.

'Arthur, how are you feeling?' said Jaws, going to his human.

'I've felt better,' said Arthur. 'But I'm glad to hear Lance has a plan.'

Lance drew a breath. 'We need to retrieve the Heart Stone. It has to be us.'

'What? That's impossible!' exclaimed Bea. 'That isn't a plan – that's a . . . fantasy!'

'We can do it,' said Lance. 'I know we can. We all have our dragons and powers now.'

'I'm in. I'll do whatever I can to undo this mess and redeem myself,' added Arthur.

Jaws looked at him. 'Arthur, I know your heart. We have hearts that match. You are a good human. If you want to go forward with this plan, I will go with you. I trust your instincts.'

'I do not know how I feel about this,' Neon joined in. 'I do not want to sneak behind Dylan's back. We should wait until the rest of the Dragon Force has returned. They will know how to deal with this.'

'You heard Dylan – he doesn't know when they'll be back!' said Lance. 'We need to protect Dragon's

Claw now and the only way we can do that is with the Heart Stone back where it belongs.'

'I'm in,' said Zoe, full of confidence as usual. 'I agree with Lance. We can do this.'

'If my human is in, so am I,' said Violet.

'Bea?' asked Lance hopefully.

Bea took a deep breath. 'Even if I do agree to go along with this bananas plan, how are we going to get out of Dragon's Claw? It's locked down!'

'Leave that to me,' said Infinity.

'But then how do we find the Swarm?' Bea went on.

'I know,' said Lance, an idea suddenly forming. 'Do you remember how Dylan said if Arthur had handed over the remote, the Labs would have been able to work out where it was transmitting to?' Everyone nodded. 'Bea, you're a whiz at molecule magic. Could you work that out too?'

'Maybe, but didn't Arthur say he threw it into the Mirage?' she asked with a frown.

'Wait right here,' said Infinity with a sly grin. 'I will be able to find it.'

'You are going to go into the Mirage?' Neon demanded.

'Infinity, are you sure?' asked Jaws.

'Even I would not dare go there,' added Violet.

'I go there all the time,' said Infinity. 'I will be back soon!' She burst through the wall of the Volcano, her four gemstones glowing.

The rest of the group stood in silence, and Lance hoped that Infinity knew what she was doing. A few minutes later, she burst back in, the remote clutched in her claws.

Bea took the remote from Infinity and held it out in her open palms, staring intently at it. For a few moments, nothing happened. And then, with a spark of electricity from Bea's fingertips, the device hopped in her hand like a kernel of corn popping. Bea's eyes widened, and another spark hit the remote, making it jump. More and more sparks flew from Bea's palms to the device until it lifted into the air, hovering in front of her. She bit her bottom lip, her eyes unblinking, and sparks of electricity began to flow through her hair, making it stand up straight.

Bea moved her hands, and the remote tilted in sync with her movements. Then she stretched her arms apart like a bird opening its wings, and the device suddenly exploded in slow motion, breaking into hundreds of pieces that froze in mid-air. She examined the fragments, flicking her fingers and moving individual parts in front of her.

'Ah-ha!' she exclaimed. Then she clapped her hands and the pieces of the remote re-joined like a puzzle putting itself together. Bea smiled as she held it out. 'Very sophisticated technology. Nothing I can't handle though.'

Arthur furrowed his brow. 'What did you do?'

'I've reversed the tracking data! Now instead of transmitting information from the remote to the Swarm, it will transmit from the Swarm, so we'll be able to track him!'

'That's amazing!' said Zoe. 'Bea, you're incredible!'

Bea tapped a button on the remote, and it projected a series of numbers in the air.

'What is that?' said Lance, frowning at the numbers.

'I know,' said Arthur suddenly. 'They're co-ordinates! It must be where the Swarm is.'

'Arthur, can you use your pathfinding skills to lead us there?' asked Lance.

Arthur touched his fingers to his temples, focusing on the numbers.

'Hold on, I'm trying to see the location in my mind . . . Ah-ha! I've got it.' Arthur grinned. It was the first time Lance had seen him smile all day. 'That must be the Swarm's lair. And it's in Dracordia. I think it will take about six hours to get there, but I can lead us.'

'And you say you can break us out of Dragon's Claw?' Neon asked Infinity.

'Yes, in the same way the three of you got into the Volcano.' Infinity's gemstones blazed.

'That's amazing, Infinity,' said Zoe.

'It truly is,' said Neon. 'Infinity, I believe you are coming into your powers in a way nobody could have predicted.'

'And I bet she has even more surprises in store for us,' said Lance proudly.

'If we are proceeding with this plan, and it seems we are, I will leave a message via flame post for Dylan so he knows we are trying to rescue the Heart Stone,' said Neon. 'Do not worry, I will enchant it so it only appears in the morning once we have gone.'

After Neon prepared the flame post, Lance looked at his sister, his friends and their dragons. 'We can do this. Together. We're going to bring back the Heart Stone and we're going to make the Dragon Force proud.'

'Let's go,' said Zoe, leaping on Violet's back.

Bea hopped on Neon and Arthur climbed on Jaws. 'We're as ready as we'll ever be,' Bea said.

'I really hope we don't die,' said Arthur.

'Don't worry,' said Lance. 'We've got our dragons, and we've got each other. Infinity, lead the way!'

The group flew out of the Volcano as one and sped towards the closed curled edge of Dragon's Claw.

'This is your moment, Infinity,' Lance said.

Infinity roared, and as she did, the claw unfurled just enough for the group to slip out, allowing them to fly into the night towards Dracordia.

Towards the Swarm.

The Nest

Following Arthur's directions, the group flew through Dracordia. Even though it was dark, the moon gave off enough light to illuminate the striking landscapes below them. From mountain ranges to great plains to floating islands, all filled with strange creatures, Lance took in everything he could, gobsmacked by what lay beyond the boundaries of Dragon's Claw.

Hours later, as day started to break, they arrived at a wall of rock that stretched high into the clouds above them.

'Are we here?' Lance asked.

'I think so,' said Arthur. 'Yes, this is the plateau the

nest rests on.' He put his hands to his temples as he'd done in the cavern and was quiet for a moment. 'We're close, but I can't find a path into where the Swarm is. I think he's at the top of this plateau though.'

'One step at a time, pathfinder,' said Bea. 'Let's get onto the plateau first.' She shot up towards the sky and disappeared into the clouds. The others quickly followed.

They flew so high and so fast that Lance felt like a rocket blasting into space. When they finally reached the top of the rock wall, the air was freezing cold and so thin it was hard to breathe. Lance peered over the top, and as expected, a long, flat plateau stretched out before him, but something else caught his eye. Squinting, he could just about make out a shimmer of gold in the distance.

'Look!' he said, pointing at it. 'Arthur, is that the Swarm's lair?'

'Yes!' said Arthur. 'That spot aligns with the co-ordinates!'

'And I can sense the Heart Stone now too,' added Infinity. 'I was not able to track it from such a distance, but now I can feel it.' She closed her eyes.

'The Heart Stone is part of Dragon's Claw, just like I am. We must return it or Dragon's Claw will collapse.'

'Infinity is right,' said Tank. 'I am not as linked to Dragon's Claw as she is, but I can feel how much it is missing the Heart Stone.'

'It is not just about Dragon's Claw,' said Violet. 'If that beetle-man has the Heart Stone, he will grow powerful enough to destroy all the New World. He must be stopped.'

Lance nodded. 'We can do this.'

'We should move on the ground,' said Neon. 'It is less likely we will be detected that way.'

The four dragons crept towards the centre of the plateau, their heart-bonded riders on their backs. Infinity changed the colour of her scales so they matched the sandy earth beneath them.

Lance gave her a pat on her neck. 'See, your power is really useful. It's great for sneaking around.'

Thank you, Lance, Infinity replied through their bond.

Soon the gold shimmer came into focus. It looked like a giant bird's nest.

'Beetles do live in nests,' Lance mused out loud. 'So this must be the Swarm's nest.'

'What're all those things crawling around the nest?' asked Bea.

Lance had been so focused on the nest itself, he hadn't noticed the hundreds of small gold creatures blending in with the sandy earth. They were the same beetles that had swarmed him and Infinity back at Dragon's Claw.

'Violet,' said Zoe, 'can you try to put the beetles to sleep? We can't take any chances. Now the Swarm has the Heart Stone, who knows how powerful he and his minions have become?'

Violet's eyes flashed and purple mist flowed out from underneath her scales as she twisted and twirled her long, slender body in the air. She flapped her many sets of wings, each moving to its own rhythm, and pushed the mist towards the beetles, covering them in purple fog.

The beetles continued to crawl around unfazed.

Violet frowned. 'They appear to be immune to my mist.'

'I'll supercharge you!' said Zoe. Violet settled on

the ground again and Zoe put her hands on her dragon's back, furrowing her brow in concentration. Flickering purple sparks of power danced over Violet's scales and into the fog.

'You two share a close bond,' said Jaws in appreciation.

'Of course we do,' said Zoe. 'But it doesn't seem to be helping us now.'

Lance saw some of the beetles had started to flutter their wings as if trying to fan away the fog, but otherwise they remained unaffected.

An idea come to Lance. 'I know! Neon, you should do the electric whip!'

'Excuse me?' said Neon.

'That cool move you did with the lava monsters where you spun round and whipped your tail to the ground sending a shockwave through the earth,' Lance replied.

'Ah,' said Neon, nodding. 'I would prefer if you did not make my battle moves sound like dance moves, but I know what you mean.'

Neon's eyes flashed and electricity covered his body as he leaped up and spun in the air. The ground shook as the dragon slammed down his tail and a green shockwave travelled across the plateau towards the beetles.

This time, the insects didn't ignore the attack. All at once, they flew into the air, like an angry swarm of bees, their wings buzzing, and headed straight towards Lance and the group.

'I think you just made them angry!' said Arthur.

'Attack!' cried Neon, shooting electricity at the swarm of beetles. But the creatures flew straight through the bolts unfazed.

Infinity, Violet and Jaws roared and let out huge blasts of fire that combined into a single column of flames and engulfed the insects. Lance breathed a sigh of relief, sure that the creatures wouldn't be able to survive the fiery blast. But his stomach dropped when the beetles shot out of the flames, flying faster towards them now, as if fuelled by the fire.

'These are powerful beetles,' said Infinity.

'You can say that again,' muttered Arthur.

The swarm was right in front of them now. Lance saw one of the beetles tuck its wings against its body and dive towards Violet, and was horrified when it shot straight through the dragon's torso. Violet let out an agonizing roar.

'No!' cried Zoe. She hunched her shoulders and clenched both her fists. Her body started to shake, vibrating so much that she looked like a blur. She split in two, then four, then eight, until suddenly there was a whole mini swarm of Zoes surrounding Violet.

Lance could see the real Zoe was still on her dragon's back, but the replica Zoes jumped up and down around Violet, waving their arms and kicking up dirt. The beetles switched their attention to the replica Zoes and away from Violet and the others. But as soon as a beetle dived through one of the clones, it would disappear with a *poof*, and soon there weren't enough Zoes left to distract the insects.

Neon screeched as a returning beetle shot through his scales. Jaws spun in the air to dodge another beetle, but one caught him in the leg. He let out an ear-splitting roar, so loud it parted the beetles in his path.

'Your roar, Jaws!' Lance yelled. 'Use your roar!'

Jaws took a giant breath, his chest expanding, and emitted a sonic blast that blew the swarm backwards. He turned and let out another blast in the other direction, clearing the beetles all around them.

'Put up a shield, Neon!' Bea yelled.

Neon's eyes flashed and an electric green dome appeared around the group.

The swarm quickly recovered from Jaws's blast and flew straight towards them again. But as soon as the beetles hit Neon's force field, a huge boom sounded as they bounced off it, unable to penetrate the shield. Neon, however, buckled under the impact and a few managed to fly in. One beetle dived in Infinity's direction, but she managed to spin out of the way just in time. Lance threw his erhu at another, knocking it back out of the force field. And Jaws lunged at a third, catching it in his teeth. There was a soft *pop* as he crunched down on the creature and swallowed it in one gulp.

'Surprisingly tasty for an insect,' he said, licking his lips.

The green dome was free of beetles once more and Violet used the opportunity to heal the group.

Her eyes flashed and a familiar mist flowed out from under her scales. Lance felt rejuvenated as he breathed it in, and he could see the wounds Neon and Jaws had sustained were healing.

'I do not know how long I can hold up this force field and keep the beetles out. It is like trying to hold a pile of sand in your hands. It is impossible not to let any grains slip through the cracks.' Neon's voice was strained with effort. 'The Swarm must have used the Heart Stone to power up his little friends.'

'You are right,' said Violet. 'It seems only Jaws's bite can pierce their shells, and there are too many of them for him to catch with his teeth.'

Neon buckled again as if holding a great weight, and a flood of beetles flew through the force field. Lance threw his erhu at them, knocking some down, and Jaws was quick to pounce on the others.

'We have to think of something fast,' said Bea. 'Neon is getting weaker. I'll try to supercharge him, but I don't know how long it will last.'

Had Lance led his friends and his sister to their doom? He was the one who had been so confident they could do this.

Infinity, I'm scared, he thought down their bond. *We shouldn't have come here.*

Do not be afraid, she thought back. *Your bravery is making everyone else feel braver too. And I feel something else. I feel something inside me awakening. I think I now know what my powers are. And it is because of you, Lance — because of your strength and kindness and how much you want to protect the others. It is making me strong.*

Infinity began to glow and started to speak aloud.

'I have always known I am linked to Dragon's Claw, and to the Heart Stone itself, but I believed all that meant was that I knew the secrets of Dragon's Claw. I had never left it before because I was too afraid. Now, with my heart-bonded human, I am not afraid. I feel braver than ever. And I can feel the Heart Stone calling to me. I think we are linked by more than just the fact we are made of the same thing. I think we can create the same thing too.' Infinity glowed brighter and brighter. 'I think I am capable of creating golden elixir.'

Lance felt his jaw drop. His dragon could create the magic that powered all of Dragon's Claw? 'Infinity, that's incredible!' he said.

Neon's eyes widened. 'It cannot be.'

'But that's the most powerful substance in the whole universe!' gasped Bea.

'Powerful and dangerous,' added Jaws. 'Are you sure it is safe?'

'There is only one way to find out,' said Violet. 'Infinity, I know you have not known me long, but I can sense in you the greatness that has been foretold. This is your moment to show your true powers.'

'It's Infinity's choice,' said Lance firmly.

'I will try,' said Infinity.

'I'll send you strength down our bond,' said Lance.

'You can do it!' cheered Zoe.

'I do not know what will happen when I make the elixir,' said Infinity.

Lance looked into his dragon's eyes. 'Whatever happens, we'll be right by your side. And with golden elixir, we'll be strong enough to get through these beetles, take on the Swarm and return the Heart Stone to Dragon's Claw.'

Infinity nodded. Then, to Lance's amazement, a golden mist began to flow from her four horns as her gemstones glowed more brightly than ever before.

Infinity raised her paws up to catch the flow of mist. It coated her paws until they contained a small pool of golden elixir.

Lance felt as if everyone was holding their breath.

'It is too potent for you to drink, Lance,' Infinity said. 'But you will feel its power through our bond when I do.'

Infinity licked the golden elixir, and her scales immediately changed to a glimmering liquid gold. Her four gemstones shone so brightly it was as if they were creating their own light, and her four horns, also now gold, grew taller. It looked as if she wore a crown of shimmering golden power.

Lance suddenly felt a burst of energy in his chest. It was too much to hold in, and the energy burst out of him. He looked down at his hands and saw they'd turned the same gold colour as Infinity. Even his super-suit and shoes had changed colour.

'Lance, are you okay?' asked Zoe, her eyes wide with fear. 'What's happening?'

Just then a stray beetle shot towards Lance, crashing into his shoulder. But instead of passing straight through him, the beetle bounced off, and its wings fluttered as it tried to regain composure.

Lance felt a power he'd never experienced before coursing through his entire body. He looked up at his sister, his friends and their dragons and grinned.

'I think the golden elixir has made me invincible.'

The Heart Stone

Lance knew it had to be him and Infinity, and only them, who went into the Swarm's nest. He turned to his friends to tell them his plan.

'Neon, you and Bea hold up the force field for as long as you can. Jaws, use your roar to keep the beetles away and chomp on any that make their way through. Arthur, try to use your pathfinding skills to map out where the beetles are going next. Zoe, distract the beetles that Jaws can't eat with your replicas. And, Violet, heal anyone who gets hurt. Infinity and I will come back as soon as we can, hopefully holding the Heart Stone.'

'No way,' said Zoe. 'I'm not letting you go in there by yourself!'

'It has to be me and Infinity,' said Lance. 'We've been powered up by golden elixir and nothing can hurt us right now. We're able to get close to the Swarm, grab the Heart Stone and come back. But if you guys go, you'll get hurt. And I can't let that happen. You all need to stay here until we come back with the Heart Stone.'

'Lance is right,' said Arthur. 'I hate to admit it, but he is.'

'Good luck, Lance and Infinity,' said Bea. 'You can do it!'

With a nod at his friends, Lance shot through the force field on Infinity's back and they raced towards the nest. He'd never felt more powerful or energized in his life. The beetles that had been unstoppable only moments ago now bounced off him and Infinity like cotton balls.

How do you think we get into the nest? Infinity asked through their bond.

We make our own entrance, Lance replied.

Infinity smiled in understanding, and they dived straight at the golden nest.

As they approached the nest's walls, Lance threw his erhu and the golden instrument crashed through the branches, easily clearing a path for them. Inside, Lance saw a large tunnel that led deep into the plateau. They flew down into the earth, their gold bodies glowing and lighting their way, and soon arrived at an enormous cavern. Lance could tell by the moving flecks of gold that the floor and walls were completely covered in beetles. There must have been millions of them.

'So we meet again,' came a voice. 'You children are just as pesky as Billy Chan and his buddies. How foolish you are for coming into my lair.' The Swarm emerged from another entrance, smiling and showing his many teeth. The Heart Stone hung on a chain round his neck. 'But how delightful for me! I've always enjoyed an early morning snack.'

Lance stared at the Swarm. He found it hard to believe this creature used to be human. 'Give us back the Heart Stone,' he demanded.

'Ha, so direct! Do you really think you can barge into my nest and demand to take my prized possession?' The Swarm fluttered his hard wings. 'I thought I had hit the jackpot when I successfully stole the Heart Stone. I need golden elixir to survive, and there is barely any left in the world. The Dragon Force is hoarding it all for themselves! But then I heard of another creature, more powerful even than me, with a hunger like no other. He wants to devour the whole of Dragon's Claw. And this creature has something even better than golden elixir, so we made a deal. I weaken Dragon's Claw by taking the Heart Stone, and he will reward me. But now I know that this little dragon can create golden elixir, what a prize you will be for my master!'

A lump formed in Lance's throat. 'What are you talking about?'

'That's right – I saw your little trick outside. I used to run the greatest technology company on the planet. I have eyes *everywhere*. I knew your group was coming here way before you could even see the plateau.' The Swarm chuckled to himself. 'My master will be here soon, and oh, will he be happy to see what I have for him!'

'Who's your master?' said Lance, a strange chill running through him.

'The most powerful creature the New World will have ever seen, and the mastermind behind all the recent attacks. You thought that was me, but even I am not powerful enough to unleash monsters across the entire globe. Soon I will be though!' The Swarm's eyes shone with a strange fervour. He looked possessed. 'The plan is perfect. Weaken the whole world. Distract the Dragon Force. Steal the Heart Stone. Prepare everything for my master. When he arrives here in the New World, all will fall before him. No human or dragon will be able to defeat him.'

In that moment, Lance heard the stars' warning song louder than ever.

'I don't know who this creature is, but I do know that the two of you aren't getting away with any of your evil plans,' said Lance, bolstered by his newfound invincibility.

Quick, Infinity, let's take back what belongs to Dragon's Claw.

Lance and Infinity flew directly at the Swarm, but he quickly shot his claws out at them, his arms stretching like elastic. Infinity swung out of the way just in time, and the claws struck the side of the cavern. The Swarm let out a cry of frustration as he retracted his claws and shot them straight back, but Lance and Infinity were ready this time, and they dodged them easily.

'Beetles, attack!' cried the Swarm.

Thousands of beetles lifted into the air and dived towards Lance and Infinity, but they only bounced off the heart-bonded pair.

'Impressive,' said the Swarm. 'But you're still no match for me.'

'We'll see about that.' Lance lunged forward on Infinity, dodging another claw attack, and pulled the Heart Stone from the Swarm's chain.

'No!' cried the Swarm. 'Give that back!' He let out a roar. 'It seems I've underestimated you, but that won't happen again. You're yet to see the true extent of my power. Back when I was Frank Albert, I was able to stretch my limbs, and now I'm the Swarm, not only can I do that, I can grow in size.' The Swarm raised his arms and started to expand. He shot another claw at Infinity.

As Infinity and Lance rolled to one side, dodging the attack, Lance felt a sharp pain in his shoulder.

He looked down and saw he was bleeding. A beetle had scraped him.

Infinity, what's happening? he thought, trying to suppress the panic in his chest.

Lance could feel Infinity's own fear through their bond. *The golden elixir must be wearing off. I thought it would last longer, but I must not have created enough.*

We have to get out of here. Now! Lance replied.

Infinity swooped towards the tunnel that had led them into the nest's cavern.

'Not so fast!' cried the Swarm, who was growing bigger by the second. He threw a claw in front of the tunnel, blocking their way. 'You're nothing without your gold elixir invincibility!'

Lance slammed his erhu onto the Swarm's claw, and the Swarm cried out in pain, stumbling backwards. Infinity breathed a burst of golden flames in the Swarm's direction, hitting him in the chest and knocking him to the ground. Lance and Infinity shot out through the tunnel.

We did it! We're getting out of here! Lance celebrated.

Suddenly, sharp cuts started to appear on his body – more beetles were puncturing his skin. The golden elixir protection was wearing off fast. He and Infinity needed to get back to Neon's force field shield as quickly as possible. The tunnel opening to the outside came into sight, but Lance felt the walls of the tunnel shake. They began to buckle and crack as if an earthquake was rocking the land, and then everything around them exploded.

Dazed and confused, it took Lance a few moments to realize what had happened. The Swarm had grown so much, he'd burst out of the cavern and the nest completely, creating an enormous crater in the centre of the plateau. The thousands of beetles that had been inside the nest were now out in the open air, so many of them that they blotted out the sky above.

Regaining their composure, Lance and Infinity didn't waste another second. They zoomed back into the force field, the Heart Stone clutched in Lance's hands.

'You did it!' cried Zoe. 'You saved the Heart Stone!'

'Not to burst everyone's bubble, but there are

thousands of beetles out there about to attack us, and the Swarm is the size of the Empire State Building,' said Arthur, sounding more than a little panicked. 'We don't stand a chance.'

'Don't say that, Arthur,' said Zoe. 'We've come this far. This is the final push!'

'Zoe, I want to remain hopeful, but I do not know how much longer I can hold this force field shield,' said Neon, sounding strained.

'The beetles are going to be the end of us,' said Arthur grimly.

'And if it's not beetles, the huge beetle-man is definitely going to seal our fate,' added Bea.

'Infinity, can you make any more golden elixir?' said Lance. 'That will help us!'

'I am trying, but I think I need to rest before I can create more. I am so sorry, Lance,' said Infinity, her voice shaking with effort.

'Don't be sorry,' said Lance. 'You've already done so much. We will think of something else!' But in truth, he was all out of ideas.

'There has to be a way out of this,' said Zoe. 'We can't let the Swarm win!'

But now that the golden elixir had worn off, Lance *didn't* know if they would be able to defeat the Swarm. And he couldn't shake off the fear that had surfaced when the Swarm had spoken of his master – a creature even more powerful and evil than him.

'Leave them alone!' Arthur suddenly yelled, running towards the edge of Neon's force field in the direction of the Swarm. 'Take me! I can give you information about Royden Enterprises' top-secret inventions. You'll have all the power you used to have at TURBO and more!'

As Arthur ran out of the force field, beetles whizzed towards him, ready to strike.

'Arthur, no!' cried Lance. 'Get back in here!'

The Swarm let out a hideous laugh and held out a claw. 'Beetles, do not harm this boy. Leave him to me.' He shot it towards Arthur and pinched him off the ground. Arthur screamed in pain. 'You're even more of a fool than I thought,' the Swarm said as he brought Arthur right up to his face. 'I have no need for Royden Enterprises' technology. I'm going to be made *immortal*.' He paused and smiled. 'You on the other hand are about to meet your end. I'm going to enjoy killing you, just like I did your father, in this very claw.' The Swarm squeezed Arthur tighter and he shrieked in pain.

'We need to do something,' said Zoe in utter panic. 'Anything.'

Lance couldn't believe Arthur had sacrificed himself, and, even worse, it had been for nothing. They needed him. He was part of their team, and they were so much stronger together. Then an idea struck him.

'We need to work as one!' Lance put the erhu on his lap. 'And music always brings people together. We have our separate heart bonds, but all eight of us – humans and dragons – are connected in some way too. To save Arthur, the rest of us need to focus on the music I'm about to play. Let it wash over you and take your powers with it.'

Lance took out his bow, closed his eyes and played from his heart. What sounded from the instrument was a battle cry. A summoning of strength and courage. When Lance opened his eyes, he saw gold mist flowing from everyone's hearts into the erhu, and he could feel their powers inside the instrument. He channelled the individual powers, each one different, like notes in a song, and he harmonized them to create a melody of togetherness and harmony. He played faster and faster, the music growing in strength, and with it so too did the united power of their group. 'Drop the force field!' he cried.

As the force field fell away, Lance turned his focus to the swarm of beetles surrounding them, and then, at the exact right moment, he released the powers in the erhu like arrows from a bow. Flashes of gold, purple, green and black shot out from the top of the instrument, creating a vortex of light, and large swaths of the insects were sucked into it like a tornado, disappearing with a sharp *pop*. Lance played until there wasn't a single beetle left in the sky.

The Swarm slammed his claws on the ground, Arthur still clutched in one of them. 'How dare you wipe out my swarm? Give me that cursed instrument and surrender, or your pathetic friend dies now!'

Lance gripped the erhu in his hands, the power from his friends still thrumming inside it. 'With pleasure,' he replied and threw it at the Swarm.

The erhu shot out of his hands like a lightning bolt

and struck the Swarm on the head before he had a chance to move. The Swarm fainted on impact and immediately began to shrink. He shrank and shrank until he was the size of a house cat, and then he became even smaller, until he was no bigger than a penny.

The group flew straight over to Arthur, who lay still on the ground next to the tiny Swarm.

'Arthur!' roared Jaws, landing next to his human and nudging him with his huge head. 'Wake up, Arthur!'

'Violet! You can heal him, right?' said Lance.

'I do not know,' Violet said. 'He is very badly injured.'

'You have to try,' said Zoe, her eyes filling with tears as she placed her hands on Violet's back. 'I'll supercharge your healing.'

Purple mist began flowing from Violet's scales towards Arthur. The tendrils wrapped around him and entered his nose before leaving out of his mouth.

Lance waited for something to happen. Anything. A twitch of an eye or a wobble of a finger. But there was nothing. Arthur didn't move.

'Arthur, you saved us,' said Lance, tears rolling

down his cheeks. 'If it weren't for you, I would've never realized I could combine our powers together.'

Zoe clapped her hands. 'Lance, that's it!'

'What?' asked Lance.

'Violet's mist can be used to both heal and hurt. Maybe your music power is the same?'

'You might be onto something!' cried Lance, now filled with fresh hope. 'Everyone, think about how much you care for Arthur.'

Lance closed his eyes and thought of his friend, then let his bow do the talking. Once again, gold mist flowed from everyone's heart into the erhu. Lance could feel the instrument filling with adoration and warmth, and he channelled it towards Arthur. Gold, purple, green and black light flowed into him, and for a moment, he lifted into the air. Lance thought he saw his friend take a breath, then his eyes fluttered and finally Arthur woke up. As he did, he fell back to the ground, but Lance and Bea moved quickly to catch him.

'Arthur! Are you okay?' asked Lance.

Arthur rubbed his head and looked around. 'I . . . I think so.'

'I can't believe you ran out of the force field into a swarm of killer beetles,' said Lance.

Arthur grinned. 'Yeah, but now look at us!'

'We make a good team,' said Bea.

Neon spat out an electric net and snared the Swarm who'd hardly moved since he'd shrunk in size. 'This despicable creature is coming back to Dragon's Claw. We should trap him in a bottle for the rest of time!'

'A better fate than he deserves,' growled Jaws.

'We'll work out what to do with the Swarm when we get back,' said Lance. 'But we need to go quickly. This isn't over.' Yes, they'd found the Heart Stone and captured the Swarm, but something was still bothering Lance. The Swarm's master was out there somewhere, and the stars' warning song still echoed in his ears.

Petrified

The mood should have been celebratory as they started the long journey back to Dragon's Claw. Not only had they achieved what they'd set out to do, Lance had discovered the depths of his power – he was able to harness others' powers to create truly magical magic. And on top of all that, Infinity had discovered her own power – she could create golden elixir and make anyone, or anything, magical. Together, he and Infinity could become invincible, even if only for a short period of time.

But as they finally drew near to Dragon's Claw, the group knew something was very, very wrong.

The stars were singing louder than ever and everyone, not just Lance and Infinity, could hear it this time.

Lance looked up and noticed the sky beginning to shift in colour from the bright blue of day to a strange dusty green. 'Are you guys seeing this?' he called out, feeling more concerned by the second.

Then came a horrific ripping sound, one Lance knew he'd remember for the rest of his days. It was a tearing, ripping sound, like something being broken that could never be repaired. The dragons roared and thrashed as the sound reverberated all around, and then it stopped as suddenly as it had started. But in the strange green sky above them, a dark shadow had appeared behind the clouds, and it was getting bigger and closer.

Neon glanced up and nearly fell out of the sky from shock. 'Jaws, do you see that?'

Jaws looked up and gave a low warning growl. 'It cannot be,' he said.

'What is it?' said Lance, even though he wasn't sure he wanted to hear the answer.

'It is too soon to say,' Violet cut in. 'We must get

back to Dragon's Claw quickly. They will hopefully know more about what is happening.'

'This is what the stars have been singing about,' whispered Infinity.

'Whatever it is, I don't like it,' said Arthur with a visible shudder.

'Me neither,' said Lance, and fear gripped his heart as they flew even faster back to Dragon's Claw.

By the time they were descending into Dragon's Claw, Lance's palms were slick with sweat. But it wasn't until he properly looked down at the place he'd already grown to love that his blood ran ice-cold. Dragon's Claw had unfurled, but it was completely empty.

'Where is everyone?' Bea asked in a panic.

'Nothing is even moving,' said Zoe. 'Not the trees or the plants or anything.'

Dragon's Claw looked as if it was made of stone, the colour bleached from the land.

'Something terrible has happened here,' said Neon.

Infinity let out a sharp cry of pain. 'Dragon's Claw is hurting,' she said. 'I can feel it.' And through their bond, Lance felt it too.

They landed quickly in the Palm, and the kids leaped off their dragons and ran around trying to find someone.

'Where has everyone gone?' cried Lance, looking in the canteen. He raced out to continue searching elsewhere, and as he turned a corner, he bit back a yell.

In front of him, barely moving, was Kronos.

'I do not have much time,' the great dragon said, his voice slow and slurred. 'Something is coming. Something that can ignite the most primal fear in living beings that they become petrified. The fear starts as a kernel in your heart, then it spreads like blood in your veins and grows until the fear itself paralyzes you. You are petrified. And it is not alone. It has an army of warriors that can also petrify. They descended on Dragon's Claw and captured everyone. I am the only one who was able to escape. I cannot fly, but I survived. The others were not so lucky. They have been taken.'

As Kronos's words sank in, Lance suddenly felt overwhelmed by the magnitude of this. All the Dragon Force was . . . gone? He closed his eyes for a moment. He had to pull himself together. He couldn't fall apart now. Then he remembered he wasn't alone. He had his dragon and his friends.

'Kronos, I have to get the others. We'll fix you! We'll work this all out.'

Kronos let out a sound that might have been a laugh. 'This cannot be fixed.'

'Anything can be fixed!' Lance called back over his shoulder. 'Just ask Bea!'

'INFINITY! VIOLET! NEON! JAWS! I FOUND KRONOS!' Lance shouted as loud as he could. 'COME THIS WAY! WE'RE BEHIND THE CANTEEN!' The dragons sped towards him, with Zoe, Bea and Arthur not far behind on foot.

'Kronos,' said Neon, his voice low and broken. 'What has happened?'

'Did the Swarm do this?' said Zoe. She stroked him between his eyes. 'You'll be okay, Kronos. We're here now, and we have the Heart Stone.'

'Everything is going to be fine,' Bea added, her voice trembling a little bit.

'No, this creature goes by the name of the Devourer,' said Kronos, his voice now even slower.

'Do you see the shadow? That is him coming to the New World. He has smelled our magic from a distant universe, and he is coming to claim it.' Kronos let out a low groan – his body was hardening into stone before their very eyes.

'There has to be something we can do!' Lance cried.

'Let me speak, while I still have time,' said Kronos. He took a deep breath and blew out a stream of ice that began to make shapes in the air. 'I would call down my stars for this story, but I am too weak. The ice will do the job though.' As Kronos spoke, pictures began to illustrate his words. 'After Dragon's Claw was locked down, Billy and the rest of the Dragon Force returned. But more monstrous creatures were appearing in the New World every hour, ones that even us dragons had never heard of.'

Lance gasped. 'The Swarm knew about those attacks! The Devourer must be the one he called his master!'

'The Swarm is not the only minion the Devourer has,' said Kronos. 'He sent others ahead of him, to ready the world for his taking, including the Petrifiers. They petrified and took the Dragon Force somewhere far, somewhere that the Devourer can feast on them all.'

Lance realized he was shaking, and he thought he might be about to throw up. Tears were streaming down Zoe's face, and he grabbed his sister's hand. At least she hadn't been here when the Petrifiers had arrived.

'How could these creatures defeat all of the Dragon Force?' demanded Jaws. 'Its members are the strongest humans and dragons in the New World.'

'They managed to catch us by surprise, and then it all happened so quickly. First the sky changed, next the Petrifiers arrived and then we saw the shadow of the Devourer.'

'And what exactly does the Devourer do?' asked Lance in a shaky voice.

'The Devourer craves magic with an insatiable appetite. Dragons battled him once, a long time ago, but he fled to a distant universe. It has taken him all this time to gnaw his way through the cosmos back to us. He is hungry for the New World's magic and thirsty for revenge. Dragon's Claw is full of so much magic, thanks to the Heart Stone, he would have caught its scent across the universe. First, he will feast on the Dragon Force, and grow stronger from its power, then he will come back for the Heart Stone and finally he will devour all the magic in the New World.' The ice images disappeared.

Lance swayed on his feet, dizzy from just thinking about the implications. But there was still more he needed to know.

'How did you escape the Petrifiers?' he said. 'If you evaded them, there must be a way we can help the others too!'

'It was luck. They collected us in a giant net and I was at the very bottom. Spark and Xing managed to push me out of the net while the Petrifiers were distracted, but they had already affected me, and I could not fly. I crashed here on the Palm, and then you returned.'

Kronos looked at Lance, Zoe, Bea and Arthur. 'You must save them. Please.' And then his face hardened into stone, and he said no more.

'Kronos!' cried Lance, pulling on the great dragon's whiskers. 'Come back! Please!'

'Violet, can you heal him?' said Zoe anxiously.

Violet shook her head. 'This is beyond my abilities.'

'Let us plant the Heart Stone,' said Neon. 'That is the only thing we can do right now to help Dragon's Claw.'

Infinity slowly pressed her snout against Kronos's frozen face. 'We will save you,' she whispered. 'All of you. We promise.'

A Seed of Hope

Infinity led them to the heart of Dragon's Claw in the centre of the Palm.

'This is where the Heart Stone should go,' she said solemnly.

But the ground was too hard for Lance to dig a hole. 'What do we do?' he cried frantically. 'We can't even put the Heart Stone back in its rightful place!'

'This is all my fault,' said a stricken Arthur.

'No, it is not,' said Jaws firmly. 'The Devourer did this.'

'But I'm the reason Dragon's Claw was weakened,' said Arthur.

'Yet you are fighting for what is right now,' said

Violet. 'Do not dwell on your mistakes. We must look to the future.'

'Put the Heart Stone down,' Infinity said to Lance. 'It does not need to be buried. Dragon's Claw will know what to do.'

With shaking hands, Lance placed the Heart Stone on the floor. To his amazement, the ground began to swallow the stone as if it were quicksand, soon vanishing from sight completely. Dragon's Claw tremored, and then, right where the Heart Stone had disappeared, the ground began to turn from stone to earth again, regaining its colour as the grass began to grow once more.

The Heart Stone was healing Dragon's Claw.

It was only a small area, but it was a start, and Lance felt a seed of hope sprout in his heart. He turned to his friends, and their dragons. 'You know what we have to do now, right?'

Zoe, Bea and Arthur looked at Lance.

'We need to save the Dragon Force and stop the Devourer,' he finished.

'You make it sound simple,' said Bea with a laugh.

'That's an impossible task,' Arthur jumped in.

'We took down the Swarm and we returned the Heart Stone. We can do this too.' As Lance spoke, he realized he meant it. They could do this. They had to.

'Yes, we can!' said Zoe with a fist pump, ever the enthusiast.

Arthur groaned. 'This pep talk is only making me grumpier. We lost, okay? We lost and now we need to hide in a cave until everything has blown over.'

'Arthur, don't take this the wrong way, but you were able to deactivate Dragon's Claw's defence system on your own,' said Bea. 'Obviously that was a terrible thing to do, but it's pretty impressive when you think about it. Imagine what you'll be capable of as part of a team.'

'And on the side of the goodies this time,' Zoe added.

'We've got each other, we've got our dragons, we've got this,' said Lance. 'We just need to take it one step at a time, like anything else.' Then he grinned and nodded at the dragons. 'Or one wing flap at a time.'

'All right, all right. Where do we start?' said Arthur.

Lance looked up at the looming shadow overhead.

'We start by examining the clues we already have, and we don't stop until we've found the Dragon Force. Without it, the New World is doomed.'

The group looked at each other and nodded. 'For Dragon Force!' cried Zoe. They all gripped each other's hands and gazed up at the changing sky, their dragons behind them, ready to take flight when they were.

Lance could hear the stars' warning song on the wind, calling to him, readying him for what was to come. And this time he wasn't going to shy away from it.

'For Dragon Force.'

ACKNOWLEDGEMENTS

Thank you for coming along with us on our newest dragon adventure! We love welcoming readers to the world of Dragon Force.

Dragon Force: Infinity's Secret would not exist without the help and support of a whole team of incredible people.

We would like to thank our amazing agent, Claire Wilson, for always leading us in the right direction and continuously believing in us. Thank you as well to Sam Coates at RCW for sending our dragons all over the world, Safae El-Ouahabi for her support and Emily Hayward-Whitlock at the Artist's Partnership.

Our dragon crew is led by the phenomenal Rachel Denwood and Amina Youssef at Simon &

Schuster Children's Books. We could not ask for better leaders of our Dragon Force team. Thank you both for everything. We got there in the end! We so appreciate you taking our dragons to even higher heights.

We would also like to thank the rest of the wonderful team at Simon & Schuster. Laura Hough, sales wizard! Dan Fricker, the marketing champion! Ellen Abernethy, PR superstar! Jesse Green, design queen!

We are very grateful to work with one of the best copyeditors in the business – Catherine Coe! Catherine, thank you for making our dragons shine. And to Leena Lane, thank you for proofreading the first Dragon Force book.

We absolutely *love* the stunning cover, and are so happy that we get to continue to work with illustrator extraordinaire, Petur Antonsson. Petur, thank you for bringing our dragons to life so beautifully. Your illustrations are perfect.

A huge thank you to all the booksellers, teachers and librarians for championing our dragon books. We'd like to especially thank Sanchita and the team at the Children's Bookshop, Muswell Hill, LJ Ireton at Waterstones Finchley Road and Rhiannon Tripp at Waterstones High Street Kensington. We'd also like to thank Waterstones for their ongoing support.

We are so grateful to our own wonderful dragon clan for their support and love – thank you especially to Jack, Cat, Jane, Stephanie, Ben P, Tom, Kiran, Anna, Kate, Samantha, Krystal, Jeni, Maarten, Dyna, Kris, KWoo, Rosi and Ben O for being such bright lights in our lives. And a special shout-out to some of our favourite little dragons – Cooper, Matilde, Lyra, Mylo, Lark, Rose and Coral.

Of course our biggest thanks goes to our parents for everything they've done for us, with special thanks to Kevin's parents, Paulus and Louisa, for watching our daughters so we could write this book! And to our own daughters, Evie and Mira – you inspire us every day to be better writers and humans. We love you.

© Olivia McDermott

KATIE & KEVIN TSANG met in 2008 while studying at the Chinese University of Hong Kong. Since then they have lived on three different continents and travelled to over 40 countries together. As well as the DRAGON REALM and DRAGON FORCE series, they are the co-writers of the young fiction series SAM WU IS NOT AFRAID (Egmont) and SPACE BLASTERS (Farshore) and Katie also writes YA as Katherine Webber.

Turn the page to read an
exclusive scene from . . .

Coming March 2024!

From the top of the Dragon Force Tower, Lance could see almost all of Dragon's Claw. The top floor functioned as a viewing tower, almost like the control room of a spaceship, with glass windows all around and a high-tech control pad along the edge.

Lance had been worried the tech wouldn't be working, but Bea's dragon, Neon, had a gift for technology and quickly managed to get it up and running. As he worked, his green horns sparked with energy and power.

'We are lucky we found and returned the Heart Stone,' said Jaws, Arthur's dragon. 'Without it, the magic that powers the Dragon Force Tower would have slowly drained away.'

That gave Lance hope. At least they had done

something right. But now, with almost all of the Dragon Force captured by the Petrifiers, and no idea where they had been taken or how they would find them, the task ahead felt overwhelming and insurmountable. They had to find and rescue Billy Chan and the rest of the team before the Devourer arrived in the New World.

Lance glanced up. It was early evening, and the sky was darkening. It still had a strange green hue to it, and the shadow they'd seen when they'd first flown back to Dragon's Claw from the Swarm's nest was getting bigger by the moment.

At least it was still a shadow, and according to the dragons, that meant the Devourer had not yet arrived but was still on his way. They had no idea when he would reach them or what else he would send ahead to continue weakening the New World in anticipation for his arrival.

'Any luck tracking the team?' said Bea anxiously, peering round Neon to gaze at the whirring and beeping control screens.

Neon shook his great head slowly. 'Look here. We can see when they were taken. All these blinking dots are the Dragon Force members and other Camp Claw recruits.'

Lance felt a lump in his throat, imagining how terrified the new recruits must have been when the Petrifiers arrived.

'They were here.' Neon traced a line with his claw. 'And then they were taken high above Dragon's Claw before they disappeared.'

'As if the sky itself swallowed them,' said Violet solemnly.

Lance shuddered. 'That doesn't mean the Devourer has already reached them and devoured them, right?'

'No, but it means his minions have hidden them somewhere and even our advanced dragon technology cannot track them. We will have to find them another way,' said Neon.

Lance looked out into the darkening night again, feeling desperate. He reached for his erhu, the two-stringed instrument given to him by his dragon, Infinity, and he began to play.

The sound that came out of the instrument was one of desperation, a cry for help. The notes built and crescendoed into a plea that sounded into the night. A plea for something, anything, that would guide them.

And then an answer came.

It was quiet at first, starting as a hum and then growing into a song of its own.

Lance recognized it. He put down his erhu and let the answering song echo all around them.

'Do you hear that?' he said.

Infinity nodded. 'I do.'

'So do I,' said Zoe.

'Me too,' added Arthur.

'It is the singing of a star,' said Infinity. 'But I cannot tell what it is saying.'

'Look!' said Lance, pointing out of the window.

Streaming down through the sky was a falling star, and as it came closer and closer, its song grew louder. The group watched in awe as the star plummeted into the inky waters of the Deep Dark, leaving a shimmering trail for a moment, before disappearing completely.

'We have to find that star,' said Lance. 'Come on!'

The group flew out of the top of the Dragon Force Tower and towards the Deep Dark lagoon. They landed on the edge and peered in. It was like staring into a pool of shadow you'd never emerge from if you fell in.

'None of us are trained to go into the Deep Dark,' said Neon. 'I myself have never been in it.'

'Nor I,' added Jaws.

'I certainly have not,' said Violet.

'Infinity?' Lance asked. Infinity was connected to Dragon's Claw in a way that none of the other dragons were; she knew its secrets and felt at home here.

Infinity paused. 'The occasional times I have been in the Deep Dark, I have found it frightening. Even more so than the Mirage.'

Lance gulped. If Infinity found the Deep Dark scary, it really must be terrifying. But he'd heard the song of the shooting star, and it was calling to them. Lance knew in his heart the star was trying to tell them something about what had happened to the Dragon Force. After all, the stars saw everything.

'Dragons,' he said, addressing all of them. 'Can you do an enchantment so the four of us –' he gestured to himself, Zoe, Bea and Arthur – 'will be able to breathe underwater?'

'Of course,' said Violet. 'Such an enchantment is simple for us dragons.'

'What about being able to see?' said Zoe, and Lance remembered that despite her bravery, his sister had always been a little afraid of the dark.

'It is called the Deep Dark for a reason,' said Jaws. 'Even the Dragon Force do not know how deep it is, and the darkness is absolute. It smothers light itself.'

'So how are we meant to find the shooting star?' said Arthur, sounding panicky. 'I don't want to swim in darkness for ever, even if I can breathe down there!'

'We will follow the sound of the song,' said Infinity. 'Even in the dark, even in the water, we will hear the star's song.'

'Just like whales who can hear each other singing in the sea,' said Bea.

'Exactly. And even the Deep Dark cannot dim the light of a star,' said Infinity. 'Or the glow of the heart bond. We will not lose each other.'

'Are you ready?' Lance asked his friends and their dragons.

They all nodded.

'Then into the Deep Dark we go,' he said, hoping he wasn't leading them to their doom.